DAM DUCHESS

SVETLANA LAVOCHKINA

Whisk(e)y Tit
VT & NYC

Published in the United States by Whisk(e)y Tit: www.whiskeytit.com. If you wish to use or reproduce all or part of this book for any means, please let the author and publisher know. You're pretty much required to, legally.

ISBN 978-0-9996215-5-4

Cover design by Pavel Gitin.

First Whisk(e)y Tit paperback edition. Previously published online by Eclectica, edited by Tom Dooley. http://www.eclectica.org.

For Pavel

Iosif Viscerionovich Stalin fancied hydropower. "The water muscle of Soviet industry," he squiggled in his notes. He summoned Mechanic Katz and the best engineers of Moscow to his study. Thrice, the word Zaporozhye sieved through his pepper-and-salt moustache.

"But we have neither technology nor qualified staff to build the Dnieper Dam," implored the best engineers in chorus, their eyes wandering from their shoes to the portrait of Lenin on the wall right above Chieftain Stalin's head.

"And what do you think, Comrade Katz?" Iosif Viscerionovich asked the Main Mechanic of Gunpowder Factory, the renowned revolutionary Haim Katz. Of all the Bolsheviks, this Katz had made the most incendiary contribution to putting an end to the old way of things. He had organized the smuggling of explosives for sieging the Tsar's Palace, for fighting at the barricades.

"I'm a simple stoker, Comrade Stalin," said Katz, "I don't know much about hydropower, but I know our Soviet workers are the best in the world. It is them who must build the dam."

"Well-ssaid, Comrade Katz," said the Chief, lighting up his pipe, "Sso be it."

The best engineers of Russia didn't dare to exchange glances.

"And who is the besst engineer of river dams in the world?" Stalin inquired.

"An A-m-merican Hugh Winter," replied the last Tsar's Minister of Industry, ex-Count Alexandrov, trying his best not to stutter.

"You ssaid it. We shall tow this Winter here across the ocean. And you, sso called engineers, incapable sycophants, will be under his command. Katz—you are appointed Ssuperintendent. Pack your suitcase, and when you are finished I will come and look at our Dam myself."

Haim Katz went pale, and the first gray hair lit up on his temple.

"Thank you for putting your communist trust in me, Comrade Stalin," he said.

Impossibly, randomly as the high whim hit, the engineers, stone-struck against the wall, knocked on the oak panels in their minds: good riddance—if anyone's head was to fall, it was this upstart head of a Katz.

"By the way, Katz," Chief added, raising himself from the table, "Don't forget to bring this posh wifey of yours with you, it's high time she was of some use to her renewed Motherland." And Iosif Viscerionovich Stalin smiled with all his poxed furrows, bidding the conference goodbye.

It is a matter of hours for the rails from both ends to meet, ready to run endless railcars with gravel for the greatest water mincer in the State of Proletarians. Shiny and taut tick the gear trains of muscles. The bone cogs click under the clock-faced chests. Men's mallet-ended arms turn madly around the shoulder pivots, bolting each second into the iron rails. Shudders rack the quarries with gritty fountains. The workers' jaws freeze in frenetic grins.

Women knead concrete with their feet. Steel buckets descend on them right out of the myopic sun, ladle the gray porridge, lift it on September rays and sway through the air to spew the brew into the mammoth bowls for whatever foundations, whatever spillways, whatever piers. Twice, thrice in a shift, a worker is carried away covered with burlap from head to feet, his chest squashed by a granite block. Once a fortnight, a drowned surveyor breaks the surface of the river. Those who disappear are rumored to have been caught in the pour of the concrete and entombed in the dam for eternity.

Along the banks stand slow oaks, wiggly willows, sprinkly limes, which long ago lost count and sequence of the steppe conquerors: the White Army or the Red, Left Socialists, Makhno gangs or Partisan volunteers. Civil War lasted a tiny but unpleasant spell of five growth rings, so the slow-timbers barely acknowledged that it was over, that the political power has firmly settled with the Bolsheviks. Listless at the fall equinox of 1929, they dazzle the river banks with their gold, as if buying themselves off any further bloodshed.

Building fever has seamlessly followed the Civil War. The dismembered country is now being stitched together by electric cables, securely welded by steel, gagged by concrete. Zaporozhye is exactly in the middle between the capital Moscow and Odessa at the Black Sea, the wild Dnieper parting the two buttocks of the banks. This backwater town suddenly promises to become the third largest city of the new empire.

CHAPTER 2.

A reporter from Moscow aims at the workers with his Kodak.

"Happier, happier! Do our Dnieper Song!" urges Darya Katz, ex-Duchess Voronchina, her gaunt outline bas-reliefing against a wall of expensive pink tuff: the future Machine Hall, a wonder of constructivist avant-garde. Her cropped hair, strawberry blonde, merges with the stone into a huge lion mane.

Man said to the River Dnieper:

I will lock you by the wall,
So that, falling from the summit, Water
tamed like wayward horse, Quickly
moves the modern vehicles, Pushing
trams and trains along.

Obediently, the workers wail the song, but the river drowns the words in its barking, froth on its muzzle, like a wolfhound bitch on heat in her father's kennels. Darya wrote the lyrics herself. She even composed the tune, and then drilled the song into the staff at long trade union meetings, with militia guards on the flanks.

It is her duty as Dnieper Dam Personnel Manager and Head of Propaganda to boost the morale on the construction site, to invent peppy slogans and write theme songs for performing at work. Her responsibility is also translating, mediating between the Superintendent and the best engineer of dams in the world.

At their first tour of the construction site, their two aged leather suitcases still unopened, her husband unfolded a carpenter's instrument kit.

"This, Darya, is a chisel. It's forced into wood to cut it. These are wrenches. We use them to provide grip and mechanical advantage in applying torque to turn objects—usually screws, nuts and bolts.

"Katz screws no wenches and drives me nuts," she mocks, with a solemn face.

In fact, Darya loves detail. If it concerned the minutest trifles of a dress cut, a frill, a breast dart, a ruffle or a hem, she would know the words with equal perfection in Russian, English and French. She could exactly tell Persian silk from Chinese, Peruvian wool from English. Fashion aside, were it poetry or fiction, she would be able to discern their minutest style nuances, capering freely within three literatures. Text memories evoke recognizable mellow tastes on her tongue. Even with the propaganda poems she scrawls for survival, she knows how to enjoy herself.

She also knows how to wield the available, palatable supply of manpower. When she met the best engineer of dams at the railway station, her inside pleasantly warmed to medium rare. At the end of a two-minute small talk, she sensed that Mr. Winter, skipping the intermediate phases, was already overcooked.

The next day in his cottage, Hugh Winter tried to coax her out of a victory nap with an enlightening hydraulic speech, corroborated by a different textbook, in English and brand new. "Near the bottom of the dam wall, Darya, there is the water intake. Gravity causes it to fall through the penstock inside the dam. At the end of the penstock there is a turbine propeller, which is turned by the moving water. The shaft from the turbine goes up into the generator, which produces the power."

Even awake, she would not be able tell a generator from a turbine. The stages of the great construction site hung in her mind in maggot abstraction, more buzzwords of the day than anything real: rock clearance, grout curtain, excavation. To her, Dnieper Dam was nothing but a monster porcupine of concrete with needles of steel.

Darya's domain before the Revolution had been the turbines of love, the rotors of desire. At the last Tsar's New Year's ball, the Pearl Hall whirled to Strauss and Chopin, rubies glistened in pink silk and sapphires in blue brocade, chandeliers tinkled with crystal icicles. Diadems, tiaras, earrings, bracelets scurried around and around. Untrained eyes would burst in their sockets unless they had a straw to hold on to, a golden straw that wouldn't get lost in the ball storm—"Who's this miracle?—Darya the Debutante." And they were all ready to throw themselves at her feet for a single waltz, for a single brush of her lock against their shoulder straps, all the male members of the diplomatic corps from Brazil to Norway, the officers from lieutenants to Generals, the courtiers from Master of Ceremony to butler blackamoors.

On his Moscow promotion tour of Zorro, Douglas Fairbanks forgot all about Mary Pickford when he saw Darya Voronchina, now deprived of title but still unmarried, in her still unpawned ball dress. Darya was more of a devotee of Rudolph Valentino types, but in 1917 Rudolph Valentino was still an obscure bit part.

Ex-Duchess was named in honor of her grandmother whom the great poet Alexander Sergeyevich Pushkin himself had loved madly. A squirt of poetry was no stranger to Darya herself—in 1913, she had published three poems in a symbolist literary magazine, Northern Lily, more due to the grace of her ivy legs around the editor's stern than to the elegance of the merits of her metrical feet.

Her ex-Excellency watches the workers just as her ancestors would watch their serfs in the fields, as if they all still belonged to her, ready to bow to the ground. For each of them, she has a file in her Personnel Manager's cabinet. Most of the employees are of virginally proletarian descent, but she knows exactly which of them are not. Former Tsar's gendarmes, priests, clerks, White Army officers—their genuine files are hidden in the second rows of the shelves. Altogether, she keeps the personnel data in artistic, deliberate disarray.

The moving mob exudes feral vigor, the same vigor that had executed the last Tsar a decade ago and married her to Mechanic Katz, a manic Bolshevik and a Jew. The Table of Ranks was abolished, and with it, all the wealth of Russian Highnesses and Graces replaced by a yelping Comrade. Here she is, Comrade Katz instead of Her Excellency, doing very well, meaning alive, unlike her colleagues, Tsarina's ladies in waiting. For now, she is safe behind the bony back of her husband, favored by the Great Helmsman Stalin at the moment.

Unhampered by coffins, the late Duke and Duchess, gun holes in their napes, would bounce in the ravine in a Moscow suburb to behold the sight of their Jewish son-in-law who had never wielded a fork in his life, of their only granddaughter who eats her snots, and, much worse, knows no word of English or French. As Darya has no idea of how to raise a child without an army of nannies and governesses, her girl is growing up like an urchin. Filthy, unkempt, little Mania hops about the site and hides in the quarry, braids draft horses' manes and romps with workers' children in the barracks. Their butts sore from mothers' spanking, the camp kids soon stopped bullying the daughter of the Personnel Director and Superintendent. Mania actually proved to be a robust playmate and an excellent food thief.

The last nails are thrashed into iron, and the rails meet. Jangling mauls followed by the workers' happy caws rack Darya with infernal vibrations. A calico dress irritates her skin with its cheap fibers—13 years have passed, but this itch is the last thing that remains unsubdued by the power of habit. The new-fangled fashion relieved one from the need of a servant, not that she hadn't learnt to do without them long ago. She is accustomed to pewter cutlery, to bad food, even to dirty language surrounding her around the clock. Now her teal eye lingers on an athletic Nikolai from the digger brigade, of Cossack descent, remotely a Rudolf Valentino type. Nikolai returns her gaze, grins cockily, more with his eyebrows than his lips. Yet undecided whether Cossacks are politically safe at the moment, Darya has placed his file in the second row of the upper shelf.

3.

The rapids roar like primus stoves. There is a baker's dozen of them, each with its own name and temperament. The little rapids are called calves, and they indeed moo in the tide. The bigger rapids are One Too Much, grinning with granite wolf's teeth, Schoolgirl, claiming the highest death toll, and Glutton, beside which, the water is not water anymore but something hard. Glutton chases the boats past itself like hair on end. The river is a chronic storm, in which each wave is forever nailed to its place, ever repeating its attritious route since the days of yore. The water leaps upwards and the locals call it thunder.

"Who the hell has given the horse rotten hay?" yells Haim Katz. He is picking at liquid horse dung with his high boot. "If this one kicks the bucket, too, you will drag the gravel on your own back. I'm not buying another horse—do you hear me, Petro slob?"

"Aye, Comrade Katz, do I not."

The stout Petro scratches his nape lazily and goes on to whip the mare.

"No, you don't, beast. I will check the hay tonight. If it's rotten, you're fired. Hear me?"

"And how well do I hear you, Comrade Katz," Petro

says, whispering quietly into his sleeve, "Fuck-a-Jew twice."

Before the revolution, Mechanic Katz learned all about cauldrons. At Revolution time, he learned all about gunpowder. Dizzy, awed with a breathtaking promotion, he gulped down all the textbooks he could find on hydroelectric stations. The principles were not difficult to grasp, but, his hair endemically catching the gray of October steppe, Katz realized that the foremost, vital knowledge he now had to acquire was about the slow hydraulics of the working masses, the mechanics of the folk gray matter. Katz had been quickly shown that gunpowder was much safer to handle than ten thousand proletarians gathered in one place, a volatile compilation from all over the huge ex-Russian Empire: peasants who ran away from forced collectivization and mandatory confiscation of crops; runaway felons seeking disguise in the crowd; soldiers of defeated Civil War armies, ruined merchants, petty nobility. Russians, Ukrainians, Poles, Mongols, Armenians, Finns, Tatars, Tajiks cross-breed in the dam nations' crucible, creating gene mosaics hitherto unseen.

At first, when the Superintendent ordered the Dam Village to be built, the living conditions were bearable but now, the quantity of workers having surged from one thousand to ten, their life became appalling, 30 to 50 people crammed in one bunkhouse, claustrophobia, hatred and brawl. Every week, due to the workers' sloppiness, some of the finished construction fragments fell down and equipment was spoiled by bad maintenance. Culprits were sought and found—or invented—and punished severely, but malpractice didn't stop.

To curb drunken carousals, Katz declared alcohol prohibition on the Dam, its results the same as in America.

The workers were not allowed to leave the premises of the construction site unless they were dismissed, and dismissal was a reason enough for an execution because it usually followed a display of sabotage or wicked negligence—incompatible with the building of the first socialist state in the world. Only one thing would give them a day off: accomplishing a heroic deed of communist labor.

The Dnieper Dam construction began with the launch of a field canteen for eight thousand lunches a day. Darya Katz's first Dam Head of Propaganda experience was a slogan poem on the poster that was printed by Dam Press and hung everywhere about the workers' camp. It depicted a Degas-style Amazon in red, soaring over a frail aproned dough-kneading housewife:

> *No slaves of home kitchen we are anymore,*
> *Machines'll do the onerous work.*
> *We women can now knead the concrete While*
> *factory kitchens roast pork.*

Superintendent Katz ordered the equipment in Germany because in the USSR no one had ever heard of large capacity field canteens. The kitchen-factory was purchased from the sale of wheat confiscated from 20 local villages, so the peasants of those local villages ate cats, dogs, grass, boots, and then each other.

Knowing much about heat, loving the heat, Katz couldn't help caressing the broad iron hips of the cooking stove. He brushed his cheek against the white noble enamel of newly delivered cauldrons, in which, if necessary, he himself could be boiled. The wise Siemens machines cut bread and vegetables, shaped meatballs, cooked, baked and did the dishes without any human help. Still, of eight thousand lunches, only three thousand were regularly consumed. Canny cooks stole half of the supplied meat, mixed cardboard into mincemeat to make up for the weight loss and then shaped the diluted meatballs smaller by another third. In this way, canny cooks' children had meatballs full-pork and free and other workers' children had a chance for full pork at the price of day's wage a pound. Horse carts delivered food on-site in thermos jars, with bluish soups reeking of carrion and cesspool, so the workers preferred to live on water and bread. It took two years of rebukes and threats, red-handed catch and firing before the Superintendent was finally able to fairly state in the kitchen inspection protocol, "Laudably rarer do surprises such as cockroaches and mice occur in the canteen food."

Meanwhile, he had to allow each worker brigade of 30 men to keep their own kitchen maid in the bunkhouse who, for 15 rubles a month, cooked edible lunches, did their laundry, and satisfied their male necessities. The latter service was not kitchen-maids' favorite part, and they kept complaining. Katz tried to move the she-cookies to a separate women's hostel for night, but then the workers sought sex off-site and returned with their pants all aflame with clap, so the Superintendent had but to reinstall the communal field wives in brigade barracks as a warrant of men's health.

Katz loved touching nice things. Gradually, this love gave place to the compulsive necessity of indiscriminate tactile intimacy with the entire construction site. The Superintendent puts his calloused hands on everything within his sight, like a royal taster, ready to earth any peril by his own life. He fumbles the gravel from the quarry, checking whether the right caliber is in the right cart for the right pier. He checks the cart wheels. He pokes mincemeat with his fingers, defining at once the ratio of cardboard in it.

Lest he faint from the miasma of a thousand proletarians' dischargers, Katz lights a strong cigarette before approaching the latrines with a bucket of chlorine. After lunch breaks, he profusely powders each hole. He ardently tries to teach the workers do that themselves, but they never learn to deem it necessary.

Whenever a new bunkhouse is built, Haim checks if the doors are hung sturdily on latches. At the beginning of each shift, he puts his nose close to the workers' faces and sniffs their breath. At midnight, he storms into the barracks with an uncharged pistol and tramples the gamblers' cards into the earth floor. He hurls moonshine bottles against the wooden walls. Returning into the Headquarters bunkhouse to his marital bed in the short hours, Katz falls asleep with his boots on. His features blatantly Jewish, his family name a caricature for a Slavic ear, the workers call him Comrade Shitpick, which is mainly to play down their fear of his short temper bursts.

4.

From the peg, Cobbler Yankel would have taken off whatever boot he was mending. He would have hurled this boot all across the room and who knows if Haim would dodge the heavy, sweat-hardened brick of leather with vicious nails sticking out of it. Had the boot spared Haim, it would have landed in Mother's challah dough.

"May your guts hang on a clothes line, fiend, I have no son anymore!" Cobbler Yankel would have hollered. "Go to that pope, he's your father now, roast rabbits with him, eat pork with him!"

"To marry a shiksa, oi-wei, shiksas are no yiddishe mamas, they don't care about children, their children run around filthy, with snots hanging to their knees," Mother Cypa would have lamented over the booted dough.

Relief was the second thing Haim felt upon seeing his street in Massandra, burnt to the framework. He recognized his home hut by the cobbler's peg sticking in the middle of what had been living room and workshop at the same time, the smell of glue still timorous within non-existent walls.

Haim had feared he would have had to explain to his parents all his present, between the curses and flights of boots, between Mother's wails. His Yiddish had become as bald as the steppe, had lost all its color on the long way to the diploma of Moscow Polytechnics. He wouldn't be able to speak Russian with his parents either because his father's Russian had never existed, not even a word had he needed to learn in his ghetto life.

As befitted a proverbial cobbler's son, boy Haim owned no boots. He wore his mother's until his Bar-Mitzvah, from then on his father's. At 18, Haim ripped the leather at the front to make space for his outgrown toes. He took his last sniff of the Black Sea and his last swim. A satchel in his hand, he left his village for a higher pitched future. Cobbler Yankel was convinced his son was going to Kherson Yeshiva, and would return to his village a freshly-baked rabbi. Mother Cypa was already bargaining for a rich bride.

Haim reached Kherson indeed—100 miles further north. He crossed over to the Christian part of the town. The same day, he had himself baptized. Against the background of Doomsday smeared naively on the wall, the pope plunged him thrice into a barrel of water, tongue-twisted the routine "In the name of the Father, the Son, and the Holy Spirit," and hung on his neck a tin cross on a rope. The pope wrote a paper testifying the Slave of God Haim's conversion to Orthodox Christianity, a passport across the otherwise Jew-impervious pale of settlement.

Haim wanted to change his last name from Katz to something more benignly Russian-sounding, but he could not afford to bribe the clerk. However, the money old Yankel had given him sufficed for buying gorgeously high leather boots. He loved to touch the swelling porcine honeycomb—so much leather, and all his to own.

It was not the abstract guilt of transgression that bothered Haim, it was the very material, cold, sap-sucking tin of the cross on his chest. So he threw it away into the gutter behind the church. He put his baptism document into the satchel and headed further north.

Now he would obtain the education he had always craved, mechanics, and where he had craved it, in Moscow no less.

5.

At the egalitarian whim of the new regime, the Moscow of 1918 didn't have more food than the province. People queued after grayish bread sold on ratio cards while the adjacent streets shuddered with barricade blasts. Gunpowder had been provided by the transgressor, and Bolshevik Haim Katz, coughing from the middle of his lungs, missed his sunny Massandra with all his bronchi.

Bread ended on an elfin young woman in blue rags of a coat. Transparent, nearly fainting, she still looked very haughty. "What is she made of?" Katz thought passing by the queue. The young woman's hair with thick plaits around her head seemed to be woven of the Black Sea sunset, her cheekbones a chalk curve. Two topazes or whatever those green gems from the Solomon Song were called, sat in the golden frame of double-rowed eyelashes. She was unlike all the women he had seen or even hastily known, neither at home, where he had fruitlessly coveted broad married moyds, nor the terse nutmeg she-things in Moscow brothels. This was an impossible, superior shiksa distilled to celestial heights. The saleswoman gloated, "No bread for blue bloods," and slammed the door of the bread truck.

Haim's food ratio as a Gunpowder Factory mechanic's was quite generous, with a herring to go with a bread loaf and an ounce of black leaf tea. Through yesterday's proletarian newspaper Zvezdá, the herring beckoned invitingly from under Haim's armpit.

Katz took his cap off. No one had ever taught him to bow to a woman, but he did. He performed a scraggy curtsy as he imagined the aristocracy practiced it, upon which the elfin woman burst into sonorous laughter.

She signaled him to follow her along the Tverskaya until they reached a pollen-colored mansion of four stories, its walls wetted by piss up to human height. At the front entrance decorated with stucco lions on both sides, a drunken groom was training a dappled horse to step up the broad marble staircase. The horse whinnied and kicked, covered in froth, and bit the groom, who only seemed to get ever more amused, laughing ever happier.

The present owners of the mansion—former grooms and janitors—did not like to use the main entrance: too formidable, too frightening. They had barred the main entrance with wooden planks, using the much more familiar servant's back door instead.

The elfess led Haim to a pantry-sized room in the basement. She bolted the door with a chair.

She cut the herring's head off with a rusty knife. She sliced the filet in tiny pieces, masterly separating the bones, and started to eat each morsel in a slow, graceful manner, as if they were at a royal banquet and she had never known what it was like to starve for a week.

"Tastes like anchovy if you close your eyes."

The kettle on the primus stove boiled. She poured out the strong tea in two thin porcelain cups, all cracked and brown inside, not rinsed for a month at least. Haim was stuck for words. Demurely, he was sucking on soaked tea leaves from his cup and then mincing them finely with his teeth. He was afraid to speak lest this uncannily authoritative woman hear his squiggly Yiddish accent.

"What is your name, gawky man?" Darya asked, "Kain, Abel, Abram?" She smiled, raising her right eyebrow. "You must have transgressed to Christianity to be here in Moscow, so where is your cross?"

From a pile on the floor, she took a handsome book with a cover of red patent leather.

Had Haim seen the dedication, "For Duke Voronchin with full respect—Ch. Dickens," he still wouldn't have known what there was to marvel at.

Joy and grief were mingled in the cup; but there were no bitter tears: for even grief itself arose so softened, and clothed in such sweet and tender recollections, that it became a solemn pleasure, and lost all character of pain.

"It's English," Darya said. "When reading Mr. Dickens back then, before all this happened, I thought he had laid the squalor too thick on the page. Now I wish I could kiss every sad passage in this book, so endearingly clean and cozy it looks to me now."

Frenzied laugh resounded in the floors above; three-storied curses followed, smashed dishes, horse neighing. Dryly, Darya commented, "The horse must have reached Father's study by now. His rooms were on the first floor."

The following day, Haim came to the pollen-colored mansion on the Tverskaya with a horsemeat sausage. He found the heating room. Knowing all about cauldrons, he heated the basement.

"Where do you come from, benefactor?"

"Massandra near Odessa," Haim cawed.

"What a coincidence—my father owned vineyards there."

Darya fished in the pantry, producing a dusty wine bottle.

"Last bottle! The Emperor's favorite wine, Massandra, vintage 1891, my birth year, grapes of fox tail sort. His Majesty preferred it to any Chateau Lafitte." She poured the wine into the same cups they had had tea in. The name on the bottle label was Lydia Liliu.

"It's after the last queen of Hawaii who ascended the throne that year," Darya explained kindly, "Father loved history more than he loved me."

Haim knew all about the Crimean sun, and he had seen fox tail grapes grow and had stolen many a cluster—especially in 1905, during the First Revolution. The village lads became so cheeky, thought they would get away with it unpunished—their mothers made claret of the stolen grapes, whose taste he still remembered. But they didn't get away, and their parents' homes were subsequently hit with a thematic pogrom: "Beat Kikes, the Spoilers of Russian Wine." Now at Darya's, Haim didn't quite perceive the difference between the fanciful royal wine and the simple, sweet nalewka at home, made of the same fox tails.

It took Haim more pains to overcome his shyness. Perched on a stool, he was fumbling his pork boots when Darya sprinkled his hands with the water from the kettle, lukewarm, and hid them under her dingy silk blouse. She made him sit down on an old calf leather armchair, once of Duke Voronchin's study, shortly before the revolution replaced by a more fashionable brand-new version from London. "Furniture has destiny, just like us," Darya said. The new chair must be moaning, maimed, seared by knives, wincing under the soldiers' asses, not at all as well off as this safe old ruin in the pantry.

"Now let me thank you properly, benefactor," Darya said. Her face assumed a wicked expression while she was dis-onioning herself of the rag layers.

Suns blazed under her armpits. A copper cloud sailed below her navel. Her skin was so thin that it seemed to Haim he could see her snaky pink intestines, scarred kidneys and taut, wine-red liver. It was as if, revealing herself so ruthlessly, she took revenge for all she had lost, her body an ingenious vortex, a theater of shadows: saddled panther, arched cross-stitch, banshee in flames. Flushing in waves under his unshaved cheeks, Haim worried that this carnal electrocution would make the whole mansion explode. He wondered if this was what love felt like.

The soldiers upstairs burst into drunken singing, "Fa-a-ther Frost, don't freeze me, don't freeze my good ho-o-rse." A female voice frilled the song with a goat trill.

Darya alit and poured some wine drops onto Haim's crotch.

"This is my French gift—consider it contraception, of which you just as well, no doubt, have no slightest idea."

With a coup de grace of her tongue, the elfess sent fallow Haim a-shudder and a-surge. In all his 28-year-old life, Haim had never felt guiltier. From then on, he would forbid her to ever touch him there and thus again.

"It's safer to be a Katz nowadays than a recognizable aristocrat," the registrar said. "Proletarian state favors international flavor, even of your variety, Comrade Bridegroom."

It cost Darya considerable effort to sign the marriage certificate with her new four-letter name.

After honeymoon, when the last Dickens was eaten by the potbelly stove, Haim Katz got a promotion to Main Mechanic of Moscow Gunpowder Factory, which respectable position entitled him to occupy the former bedroom of Mother Duchess in the pollen-colored mansion. Since there was no table, they ate their bread and herring in bed.

6.

Since time immemorial, the hallmark hairstyle of the Cossacks has been the world-unequaled, eccentric herring tail—a streak of hair growing out of the pate of the otherwise bald scalp. But now it doesn't befit the Soviet proletarians to show off, so Petro is just shaven completely bald, with numerous scratches on his pate, and Nikolai sports a bowl-cut.

"When will you stop forcing me to dig? It's fine in summer but now it's gettin' cold," Petro moans. "We have ploughed the whole river bank from rapids to reed beds and found nothing but crags. It's all a fairy-tale anyway."

"No, it isn't a fairy tale, freeze-ass! Cossack Kupa next door came back to the village with a cart full of gold! Why do you think we've come here, to work for dam Soviets and Comrade Stalin? We are just under disguise here and must not forget our big task."

"Let's go to sleep," asks Petro.

"Stay on task, pooch—my dad said willow," urges on Nikolai.

"Mine said lime," claims Petro, yawning.

"I bet you won't tell the difference, dunce, because your dad made you with a moonshine-washed pickle."

"Don't you say so or I'll beat you up," Petro is offended.

"You won't because your granddad made your dad with a pepper from horilka. Every dog in our village knows this."

"No, he didn't. My granddad was the strongest Cossack in Zaporozhye, and he could slay a hedgehog with his naked arse."

"The devil shat, and your granddad ate!"

The family lore debate went on until the stars strew the September sky: curfew time.

From generation to generation, the stories of Cossack treasures, custom-made for each family, were passed and passed on from father to son in great secret, and the daredevils set off to find the ancestral vaults. Sometimes the Cossacks buried coins, muskets, bejeweled swords in the Dnieper, but the river mass, now raised by the Dam, washed them away beyond retrieval.

"To dig in the dusk is stupid," complains Petro. "We must earn a day off, and to earn a day off we must do something heroic."

"Now this is a good one: heroic! Who taught you this word? But for once in your life, you're right. Maybe your dad made you with a big eggplant, after all."

Nikolai straightens himself out, stretches, and puts his spade on his shoulder. The happy Petro repeats Nikolai's movements in wonderful precision.

"You know how this Propaganda fox looked at me today?" Nikolai says. "She fancies me a lot. I bet wants to sleep with me! They say she was a real duchess. I wonder how it is to screw a duchess!—never had one in my life."

"Nor did I," mumbled Petro, yawning full throat. "But our cookie Masha isn't bad either."

"Cookie Masha belongs to all diggers, even to you. She's just a communal night pot."

The men trample the foliage towards the camp, where they share their bunkhouse with 30 more diggers, bedbugs having made them all true blood brothers.

"Ple-e-ase not two at a time," squeaks Masha, "you'll tear me apart."

7.

"I have harnessed Horseshoe Rapids, Darr," Hugh Winter says, his finger deep-busy under Darya's mound of Venus. "Yah, I worked at Muscle Shoals Dam, in Alabama, at Keokuk Dam, I subdued the Mississippi, and even as far as Aswan Dam in Egypt, Darr, did I get, but never, never have I seen such an antipodean folk as yours. Your people arr morr wicked than niggers. They don't know a monkey from a wrench, but what brilliant heads, as if rinsed clear by moonshine!"

Darya reclines on the right side of the Simmons bed. Her chin is propped on her elbow. She is submerged in studying Hugh's bedside table. On its top, a letter of complaint:

> *Attn. Superintendent Katz: Herewith I am informing you of my deep and indignant discontent at the food I am catered at the canteen: no white bread, no coffee at 6 AM, and the omelet is full of egg shells. Having suffered this for a year without complaining, I therefore demand a personal housekeeper with cook qualifications, and personal delivery of white bread.*

Lifeless dam drafts, a year's old Life Magazine with

Campbells' Tomato Soup advertisement splashed across the middle page. The call to "Lift this soup to your lips" manages to water her mouth sure enough, a brew the color of home theatre blood she would have been sick at in old times.

"It was when you were down with a flu and couldn't translate for me. Your engineers prepared a pit, Darr. Your diggers dug it for a very, very heavy piece of equipment. Then comes the equipment, and they are stumped. There isn't a crane for miles that could carry such a weight, in the middle of your steppes, Darr, and nothing to make a lash-up from. Your Engineer Alexandrov is agape, and your husband stands with a most forlorn, angry cockroach expression on his face. Your foremen babble something about positioning the heavy equipment on bed bolts, and fuss, and stumble, and faint into insipid murmur."

Under the Life Magazine, there is a new hardcover book by one Ernest Hemingway, The Sun Also Rises. Darya shuffles through the pages—Paris, Pamplona, New York, San Sebastian, names all like jingles of light, far from the steppe sleet. She sniffs the fresh ink wind the pages make between her fingers. Winter's relentless finger drill has rubbed her sore.

"Meanwhile, your diggers buzz and buzz among themselves. They push a man forward, quite a cunning face, sort of Slavic Rudolph Valentino."

At the mention of Rudolph Valentino, Hugh's fingers get very moist—this is the only thing Darya perceives from the ongoing story.

"Beside him, a fat, flour-cheeked clown of a friend. I have seen them beforr. They can dig and dig in any weather. They pack their pants full of dirt as if all gold of Klondike had been transported here, into this dull gray steppe. So the clown friend says, "If ya want to get this big schlong into this hole softly—ha-ha, then we'll help ya along. We do, ya watch!"

The engineers and your Katz get nervous, but I signal the diggers to get storrted. And the fat man and the Rudolph Valentino man fill the pit with cakes of ice, Darr, just plain ice lying around everywhere, and skid the thing into position. Then they sit down proudly and light their awful roll-ups."

The "Sun Also Rises" book starts with a rant about a weakling Cohn that adds up to Darya's drowsiness from Winter's tale. But out of reverence to the word "Paris," Darya resolves to read on, later, a bit later, when her bedmate's voice falls silent, which is not to be expected so soon.

"Your engineers are flush-red and ashamed, your husband Katz is bursting with contradicting emotions—"Didn't I tell you the Soviet workers are the best in the world?" Engineer Alexandrov translates for me, and Mr. Katz scowls at Mr. Alexandrov derisively, and to me, he gives a wry smile—does he know of us, Darr?"

In fact, it has never occurred to Darya to wonder.

"Anyhoo, the ice melts and the diggers just pump the water as fast as it gathers," Hugh drawled on. "The cunning man and the fat clown man said they are of an ancient warrior race, Cassocks, or Cusacks, I forget."

Darya curls herself into a fetus and sighs. The best engineer of dams cranes himself over the curled Ex-Duchess, digging his nose into her red curls. She buries her head in a pillow with a sweet murmur. Hugh tries to gentle-soft into Comrade Katz, but she is fast asleep.

8.

The sandy beach patch further down the river is called "The Caucasus." It overlooks the Glutton Rapid. Gypsies camp here, Superintendent's nightmare, neither belonging to the construction site nor quite aloof from it. They live in patched tents, make moonshine from incredible stuff, they say, even from feces.

Darya has come to the gypsy camp at sunset. The Dnieper rolls down like a Turkish carpet, with stories undulating in indigo and red, the rapids still puncturing the water texture far up.

The gypsies crouch on the bank, men lazily smoking, women hanging rags on ropes stretched from an oak to a lime. A curly favorite of the camp, young rom Román, plucks at his seven-stringed guitar with a plangent melody. The song sets female shoulders and rears into dreamy swaying. Gaunt clothes flap on the rope lines stretched between a willow and a lime, like limp pheasants. Sticks merry-go-round in the soup cauldrons, their steam relating the saga of today's lucky food hunt, of a rabbit ensnared.

"Ai-ne-ne-ne—a high visit do we get!" Rom Román swaps from Romani into Russian. The women turn around, pinning the gaunt, pink-haired apparition with their black irises.

"Catch me four foxes," orders Darya without a greeting.

"Let us better catch you two dozens of hares," says the handsome Román, "hare meat a-snare is better."

"No you queer ones, with meat, you do what you like. I need the fur."

"We're not skinners, Lady Red Wisp, we're knackers and horse stealers."

Darya proffers Blacksmith Stepán, the elder, a hundred rubles—"This will help you along." Half her salary and twice a worker's wage. The gypsies grin—the money will feed them through winter.

"Then we shall, aye we shall skin hides for thee, wispy damsel."

An old gypsy woman catches Darya's hand, her skirts releasing the jailed air, decade-old, her necklaces jingling.

"Let me read thy fate, thou fine one, thou chosen one! Thin hand, blue blood, lamentable, doomed fate!"

"Remove thee, I don't want to know anything," Darya shakes off the darkness of the gypsy's grip.

"Ai-ne-ne-ne!" the whole camp bursts into singing in the Romani language which is beyond Darya's competence. "Aye, bushy tailed foxes shall we catch, cunning foxes for her gallows loop!"

Rom Román casts off his shirt and pants, his nakedness wiry and taut but devoid of sharpness, warm and inviting, like a male Kama Sutra figure. To unanimous Roma cheering, he runs up, whipping the fine sand. His body loses its skeleton and liquefies into ember ink. As if led by a swift pen, it flourishes a cursive m with an elegant loop in the middle, ending in suspension points. Without so much as a shiver, Rom Roman plunges into October water.

Román twirls his way up to Glutton Rapid, by now half-drowned by the progressing dam but still a dangerous maelstrom. He emerges out of the wave froth, nymph-fondled, and presses his front into the granite rock, as if it were a cast to eternize his deed.

Not once did Alexander Sergeyevich boast all over Moscow and St. Petersburg that he had managed to reach the terrible Dnieper's Glutton Rapid at the summer solstice of 1821, petrifying two drunken Cossacks who took him for a devil. But Rom Román does not know of poet Pushkin, and hence, of any rival. He is the first human-being Darya has ever seen to cope with the tide—in cold water, way past fall equinox.

9.

God-awfully tasteless, pathetic contraption with a skewed tennis court: still, Hugh Winter's cottage is the closest one can get to human comfort at the Dnieper. It is more because of the hot water in the bathtub that Darya visits the best engineer of dams in the world at lunch breaks. She has been frequenting him since they first met at the headquarters assembly, on the day of their arrival to Zaporozhye.

Hugh Winter has built many dams. He knows all about dams. He loves dams with all his turbine heart. He adores water in all states of matter, whether it is ice diamonds in whisky, or cold rivers born in heavy clouds.

Winter's physique is clean, the smooth trinity of chest, chin and broadcloth. He is well-built, blindingly white-teethed. He sports a ring with a square topaz, a trophy from Egypt, where he built the Aswan Dam, and a pipe. Immune to any climate, tempered in Minnesota since birth, his Fahrenheit vigor range is from minus 60 to plus 120.

Mr. Winter is in excellent hydraulic condition for his late 40s. He sees bed as a cotton lake pregnant with electricity. Non-stop powerhouse, he spindles love waters through the vanes of his fingers. He surveys the wet cavity, erects a grout curtain; he stops leakage and checks the flood pressure with genuine, meticulous instrumentality.

After each hydraulic siesta, Darya Katz feels like a spillway pier stuffed with concrete, but the hot aftermath bath dissolves this square heaviness. Pedantic in shaving, Winter brought a lifelong supply of Gillette razors and Nennen shaving cream, this American apparel of dubious taste.

No. 4711 was the eau de cologne their Moscow butler used to drink when he ran out of vodka. It is ironic that Hugh Winter should smell of it, the tedious whiff of rosemary, tangerine, and thyme. "Haberdashery rooster," father Duke would have said indulgently. But now, compared to the dam stench, this numbered water equals a remote morning of Provence.

When Darya first stepped onto the living-room rug, she nearly wept at the impotent cacophony of the carpet pattern, in a clash with the gaudy flowered sofa, and at another clash with the linoleum. The Simmons bed was ugly in its graceline tubing, but the Liberty mattress was soothing enough for her back, after she had been rose-winded by the best engineer of dams, in all directions.

The only pleasant piece of furniture in the whole house is a walnut cupboard encasing a Victrola Talking Machine, gold-plated, with contrasting veneer and stains, its legs ornate and curved. Winter must have brought the hulk all the way from America.

In the summer of 1912, Father Duke had adamantly refused to purchase the very same model of Victrola in the first gramophone shop in London on Oxford Street, despite Darya's gentle pleading, despite Mother's nervous

French imploring. It was in no way the 300 pounds plus shipment expenses that the store owner requested (the gentleman even courteously offered a gorgeous set of classical music records to go with the machine for free).

"As long as I can afford live musicians, I won't be fed this squeaking surrogate," Duke Voronchin said, turning on his heels towards the exit, Darya, Mother, and Mother's peach-colored pug on a shaking lead pouting sternly after him. The shop owner opened the door for them personally, courteously, without any trace of disappointment on his face encoded by generations of Anglo-Saxon chivalry.

To prove the superiority of live manpower over mere mechanics, upon their return in St. Petersburg, Father hired a chamber orchestra on a daily basis to facilitate digestion's waiting on appetite. In the parlor, no matter whether for a crowd of guests or just for them three, the musicians played symphonies and concertos, sonatas, and fugues à la carte.

In Winter's living room, Darya opens the shiny doors for the record shelves. Only treacle pulp trash on motley labels: "Moonlight in Jungleland," the babble of "Bear's Oil," the agricultural "Forosetta-Tarantella," and such. No classical music at all, the least vulgar of all the records being "John Brown's Body," whose melody she lukewarm-liked. She thought it might be used for the Great Dam Hymn in due time when it was finished, if it was ever to be finished.

To accompany their preparatory manual phase, Winter does try to put on Moonlight for "mellow mood."

"If you ever want to see what's under this dress, prithee turn the machine off at once," snaps Darya, "unless you keep Tchaikovsky or Chopin in a hidden nook of this cupboard."

"Do they sing 'Moonlight' be'er?" Hugh asks.

It would have been a young noblewoman's principle to leave indignantly after this phrase, but an aging ex-duchess cannot afford it.

"I say, Winter, you don't need your grand salary here at all, do you?" Darya asks, approaching his privates in a slow spell of concentric circles. "What do you spend it on, tobacco?"

"Yah—and very bad tobacco it is," Hugh confirms.

Hugh Winter buys the smokes at Torgsin, a special, well-guarded store for dam authorities at the outskirts of the construction site, away from hungry workers' eyes.

"Do you want me to stay with you?" Darya asks. "Do you want me to go to America with you?"

Hugh is actually a little a-fancy with Darya. At 48, his children grown up, his wife wilted and ever tetchier every time he returns from another long foreign sojourn, he could quite well do with a new consort, and a very refreshing species at that. He fears her feral daughter a little, but this creature has a father she could stay with, after all. There is a grand, eccentric style in this Russian woman he has never met on any continent. He even believes her having belonged to aristocracy, whether a duchess or not, this depends on the height of her ability for artistic exaggeration, which he can't measure, but it doesn't matter much. Another asset is much more important—Darr's deftness in bed matters—oh, what ticklish fever does she send upon his penstocks, especially this swooning, encircling conquest she conducts so well, the slight tease of sharp teeth, tantalizing but never painful.

"Why do you not borrow me, say, two thousand dollars?" Darr asks Hugh's navel. "My family jewels are safe in the Swiss bank, but I have no access to them now from the Soviet Union. Consider it an investment: I will bribe the foreign minister, and he will issue a visa for me. Then I'll retrieve my jewels and you will have your money back—with me as cream on top."

"Oh, geez, Darr, this… is a very… difficult decision," Hugh gasps, but in a second, he is already defeated and limp.

Foreign specialists are screened from the Soviet life as much as possible. What Hugh Winter does not know is that attempted bribes yield capital punishment. Such are the new laws with the Great Helmsman Stalin at the steer. An ex-duchess would never be allowed to go abroad, even a thousand times less than a simple, modest proletarian person.

Darya possesses nothing at all. Her jewels and her Swiss bank account papers had been duly confiscated from their St. Petersburg house, before her parents took refuge to the Moscow pollen mansion, where they were greeted by an executive troop, loaded onto a truck and taken to a suburban forest with a wide ravine.

On the porch, Hugh's newly-employed housemaid gives Comrade Katz a wicked glance. This dun she-dungbeetle is apparently in love with her master, one needn't wear eyeglasses to notice that.

10.

Alone in the evening, by the kerosene lamp in their Dam Headquarters bedroom, which is just a bigger and cleaner bunkhouse of two rooms, Darya re-opens The Sun Also Rises by Ernest Hemingway. The other day, she snatched it brusquely off Hugh's bedside table, along with a roll of green banknotes, deaf to his sleepy "Darr—but I haven't finished it yet!"

"You mean you haven't storrted it yet I suppose," Darya snapped, mocking his Minnesotan accent.

Though a very second-rate spa for her wilting Oxford English, the Sun Also Rising promises to be entertaining enough, but soon Darya realizes it is a very wrong book to read. Fury gathers in a furrow between her eyebrows, envy devours her up to the pink roots of her hair. At 38, Darya Katz is living off the last stocks of her beauty in the Ukrainian steppe, slowly shriveling for ghastly food—Oh, had she only listened to Coco, had she accepted that job! In the Paris of 1916, they were all dining at the Ritz when Mademoiselle Chanel said, "Let the belle Daryá stay here in Paris, Duc. She'll be safe from this révolution russe of yours."

"Over my dead body!" Father, still Grade One in the

Table of Ranks, hit his cane on the parquet, impaling the wood like a bullet, so that the startled waiter spilled a tureen of consommé on Mother Duchess' peach-colored pug. He would never allow his daughter to work, the more so, work as a tart—yes, a model is a tart. Had she stepped over his living body, she would still be the adored, fashionable, mysterious Russian Duchesse, frequenting the same Parisian cafés as that unadulterated tart Brett, and unlike Brett, she would have to be strangled to sleep with that Cohn. Her eyes without a single crinkle, she would soar over Pamplona in Spanish heat and would definitely flash the curves of her wit besides the hull of a racing yacht in her jersey. If marry at all, why not the best ones—Picasso, Bréton or Dalí—she could have rendered any of them love-berserk. In this case, she would probably have to make the concession of getting used to this new-fangled jazz music, should that have proved unavoidable.

The young torero has won another fight with Brett's kerchief on his spear, but she seems to love her gelded Jake nevertheless. She knows what love feels like. Haim Katz, although well-endowed, is at present as much use in bed as Hemingway's narrator. Their differences, grown insurmountable within a decade and now topped by this construction site, licked off the last remnants of mutual desire. All Haim thought of was how Comrade Stalin would find the Great Dam—like lice, petty troubles infested his side of their barren bed. The revolution deprived Darya more than of jewels, title, or fortune. It had apparently swallowed the prince who had been predestined for her before they had a chance to meet.

The sun is high in San Sebastian, the book is nearing its end. Jake has just returned from a swim in the bay, serene and refreshed. He has sat down in an easy chair to catch up on French sporting life when the concierge comes out with a blue envelope, an SOS from the tart Brett who is "rather in trouble." But before Jake can tip the concierge, the door of Dam Headquarters bedroom flings open.

"Le-e-ave me alone, damn Dad!" yells Mania, drawn by the ear. The wall clock shows midnight. Father Katz throws the urchin on the bed.

"Our Excellency washes herself three times a day—after each mating—but it's below her dignity to clean her daughter's nose. It is below her dignity to teach her daughter to read. I'm fed up, do you hear, you prodigal thing? I'm fucking fed up! Either you take care of her, or I'll send her away to the orphanage."

Katz takes a hot water kettle from the primus stove and starts wiping Mania with a wet rag.

"I always knew you were crooked. My mother would have spit at you, God make her grave soft as down," the Superintendent goes on from some bleak distance, almost inaudible in Madrid-bound Sud Express, where Jake and Darya have breakfast in the car, watching the rock and pine country between Avila and Escorial.

"I cannot even pronounce what my father would have said about you in five languages, God rest him in his ravine," Darya replies routinely, without much verve.

"Lice! She is as infested with lice as you with your foreign words, and with foreign spawn!"

Haim dilutes some kerosene with water and tumbles it down on Mania's crown.

"AAA-r-rgh fuck you fuck you!" yells the child in a Mowgli voice.

Haim presses his daughter's head between his knees and starts to cut off the sizzling tresses with carpenter's scissors. Then he shaves her head clean with his razor.

Darya puts the book aside and takes up her notebook and her fountain pen. She proceeds to compose the next song to drill into the workers:

My Zap in the steppes,
Stronghold of the country,
On sinews and blood,
On the lice of new times.

It dawned on her Head of Propaganda to give the bedraggled name of Zaporozhye a radical shave: Zap—a neologism, a quicksilver invention. With a biting spur of a nickname, the town, too, will be made over forever.

Haim is fast asleep, prone on the bed with his boots on. Bald Mania snuffles peacefully into her first dreams, clenching her father's jacket, his ear between her teeth, her face a muddy puddle. Of course, Darya corrects "lice" to "verve" before extinguishing the kerosene lamp.

11.

The dam stock clerk Aaron Garlic spent the evening combing the severed dark brown tresses, gleaning pearls after tiny pearls of dead louse eggs from each hair. He washed the redeemed locks in a bowl with industrial soap, poured a generous amount of hydrogen peroxide from the dam infirmary. The workers never bothered to come for disinfecting wounds—it took a broken spine or typhus to go to the feldsher, so Aaron swapped a woolen blanket for a bottle. In a quarter of an hour, Aaron conjured up some bleached fleece, lifeless tow. He rinsed the locks in a zinc bucket, then made very strong chamomile tea, and poured a splash of sunflower oil into the bowl. He put the tresses onto a gray linen pillowcase. In the morning, he yielded a dry, long and pristine golden mane fit for a princess.

Head of Personnel Department, a fountain-pin of a woman, had descended upon him like a curt hurricane. Without a greeting, she demanded, "Make a doll for my daughter: let's see if you are as deft as your file says. And take this for stuffing pillows." In a burlap sack, she gave him her daughter's hair, unaware of its value.

"At your Comradeous pleasure," Aaron bowed in an

old-fashioned way. He had seen this daughter, who certainly did not look as if she was in need of a doll. Neither had it ever occurred to her mother to bother to supply her with whatever toys. His wife Shoora's hair rose at the sight of this urchin. She tried to keep their little children Dod and Sheila well away from the wild thing.

Forbidding himself to even half-inquire what the real purpose behind the doll commission was, Aaron greeted his task with enthusiasm, for it was a miniature replica of his vocation.

In separate tin bowls, Garlic dissolved permanganic acid usually used for bathing newborn dam babies. Into the acid, he put a quarter of a gray woolen army blanket and five drops of blue ink—where half a linen bed sheet was put to soak.

On the bank, Aaron picked some clay that he mixed with chalk. On the way back to the warehouse, at dusk, he passed the Machine Hall and with a pocket knife scraped some precious pink tuff into wrapping paper, to make the whitish clay pink (under the threat of capital punishment, it was strictly forbidden to touch those sacred walls).

Aaron kneaded and sculpted until he finished the high cheek-boned, Greek-nosed head of a princess, then the elegant, small hands and feet. He smashed a blue glass vial and filed two shards with a rasp until he had perfectly round, cloudy coins for the doll's eyes.

When the clay face was still very soft, he cut five millimeters off a pitch-black shoe brush, curled them into the eyelash form with glue, and stuck, one by one around the shoe-polish- outlined fair almonds, the eyelashes, fairy-tale long, in a startling contrast with the blonde hair.

He decorated the frock and the petticoat with infinitesimal shrapnel bullets that were still in abundance everywhere on the ground, ten years after the civil war; the "ermine" mantle, knitted of cotton wool he had spun with his fingers through an adder stone the size of a thumb nail, around a rolling pin—fluffily, not too tight. Into it, he wove shiny zinc shavings at the edges for precious highlights.

Aaron stuffed the doll with the Dnieper sand.

Of wire, he made the doll crinoline, and embroidered the blue hem of the frock with a complex, majestic pattern. Little leather shoes—he tanned them blue and sewed buckles on them.

"This doll does not look proletarian at all, Comrade Garlic," says Darya Katz. How will you explain that?"

"The doll was not intended to be proletarian in the least," Aaron replies.

"Are you not afraid I will fire you for ideological incompatibility?" Head of Propaganda asks.

"Madame sans merci, I can't help it," he smiles, "but you yourself you look no less than a pure countess."

Mania has kept to bed for a week—her health is excellent, but having to parade her bald head in the dam camp would shame her red and purple. Lest the children renew their taunting with new nicknames worse than hell, she is determined to stay in the bunkhouse until her hair grows at least to the length of a boy's.

At the sight of a blond doll in princess attire, Mania utters a Bagheera purr of astonishment. She has never received presents, and here is a whole fortune, a bomb of femininity: unknown, gorgeous, unexplored hutches of awe and love.

Mania cannot name her doll. She is ashamed to show her adoration before her mother and pretends not to care about the gift, but involuntarily, from her 11-year-old chest ascends a delighted gasp. At the same time, from her womb blotches down, precocious, the first clot of blood. Too proud to ask her mother about it, she thinks she is going to die.

Mania hides the doll under her mattress so that nobody will steal the princess. In the evening, thanks to camp teens, she knows all about menarche, in dam-adapted version. At night, she puts the doll under her dingy singlet, muttering indiscernible half-endearments, half-curses. She smells the chamomile hair, the garments, she checks if the doll has got breasts—it has, sand-filled, under its petticoat! She looks under the crinoline. The lap is inscrutable, undetectable. Mania imagines it is there, and wonders if it will ever bleed.

12.

Rosa Garlic has never seen such a beautiful cottage—all for Mister Winter alone. Rosa grew up sharing a room with ten siblings, so the house seemed to her almost unbearably spacious—she was afraid to lose her wits in it, afraid they would get spilled all across the living-room, the kitchen, the bathroom, the bedroom—all in all, as large as their ghetto synagogue before the pogrom.

Iosif Viscerionovich Stalin had ordered the American Mr. Winter to feel at home on the Dnieper Dam construction site. Because no one actually knew what it meant for Mr. Winter to feel at home, the reasonable plan would have been to provide the best engineer of dams with a typically American cottage at the Dnieper. The Minister-Counselor of the Soviet Embassy in Washington had his secretaries conduct much courteous telephoning and industrious research. As a result, they discovered the Mail Order Catalog of Sears, Roebuck and Co., which provided building kits for entire houses.

In the spring of 1928, the "Winona" Sears Home Kit was ordered from Chicago at the price of $1,998 plus $1,000 transatlantic shipment. Truth to tell, the decisive factor in choosing the house was neither technical characteristics nor the money. Having researched into the biography of the best engineer of dams, Minister Counselor finally picked up the house because it bore the name of Hugh Winter's hometown.

Fifty thousand pounds, 30 thousand assembling pieces: beams, oak flooring, walls, nails, hinges, paint, shingles, doorknobs, downspouts, plumbing pipes, electrical wiring and light fixtures, mantelpiece, refrigerator, central heating, flush toilet, tap-twinkling sink, a bathtub of porcelain—all screaming white. In a month, the "Winona" alighted in Odessa, from a tanker and onto a cargo train, where she sprawled herself in two boxcars. At the final destination of Zaporozhye, 50 horse carts brought her to the Dnieper—not once were the elegant body parts dropped and picked up from the dusty road.

It should have taken only one carpenter to assemble the "Winona," the instruction had assured, but it probably meant one American carpenter. In Zaporozhye, it took all the horses and the dam carpenter brigade a week to marvel at the foreign mogul and get to know the tool kit that, in its shiny dizzying variety, rather resembled a set of surgical instruments, and another month to interpret the manual. Then followed a year soaked in the rich sauce of curses, of fitting and misfitting, erecting and dismal dismounting, before the "Winona" rose out of carpenter sweat and horse froth in its seminal design—fortunately, only slightly birth-shocked: the front porch grinned a bit askance, the white paint lay on the beams in drunken bulges, and the toilet seat wiggled about skittishly whenever Winter perched himself upon it.

At first, Rosa was scared to death of a monstrous hoover (with the shipping charges, the price of Village Balabino's wheat), but then she learned to operate it. It was much faster than a besom. Now she loved wielding it, gliding along the vast stretches of the gleaming azure floor with interesting patterns of red lilies on it. Rosa changed the filters regularly, each filter the price of a rye sack.

The workers had covered all the oak floorboards with linoleum—what they thought was very fashionable—oak was considered out of date, it grew everywhere, and all the bunkhouses as well as coffins were made of oak boards.

At the ironing board, Rosa brushed her cheek along each of the blue, white, pearl gray cotton lakes of Winter's shirts. Without a ruler, she could fold them in geometrical perfection—the length and the width could serve as units of measurement in their own right. Timidly, she folded his boxer shorts, too, feeling almost a sinner when smoothing the middle seam.

Sometimes Rosa would watch Mr. Winter working at his sumptuous drawing board. He would only pause to wind the handle in the side of a varnished wooden cupboard crowned with a huge shiny bindweed head. With its diamond sting, a golden wasp meticulously licked lovely music off a stiff black pancake, always jumping up with a satiated burp before it touched the bright marmalade topping in the middle. Mr. Winter had many black singing pancakes in his varnished cupboard, each sitting in a paper jacket with a round slot in the middle, to display a different sort of marmalade on each. Mr. Winter's favorites were persimmon, cherry, and blackcurrant: it was them he put on for the greedy golden wasp to crawl upon the most often. The persimmon voice was thick, sweet, and nightly. The cherry sounded funny, monkey-clowney, and the blackcurrant whirled, hovered in an immodest dance, men and women touching each other, no less, Rosa imagined, than by shoulders and waist!

On the first day of her employment, Mister Winter led Rosa through the house, pointing at objects and naming them in English. His voice sounded like a leonine song of roaring magic, the wavy hallmark of the best tamer of rivers in the world.

Illiterate Rosa tried to build memory hooks. She repeated, diligently, "taible," following the phonetic asymptote with Yiddish "tish," "chair" with "shtul." Hugh's mother was German, as was the lingua franca of his childhood home, his father Norwegian. To compensate the loss of the native tongue for her husband, Hugh's mother cooked only and exclusively Norwegian food, having learnt the recipes from her blonde mountain of a mother-in-law: spinach soup, nutmeg cabbage rolls, and the unforgettable, fragile Christmas krumkake—waffle cones imprinted with fine ornaments, a whiff of cardamom about them. Blurred but still recognizable, Yiddish sent the long-dried German language tributary in motion, awakening Hugh's rusty soul of a Teuton. With a clumsy tongue, he asked Rosa about her life and about the Soviet Union, but she was unable to talk politics, ignorant of even the simple things. She only knew that the Great Helmsman Stalin was the fairest, the wisest man in the world, and the friend of all nations.

Rosa was conceived to be a perfect Jewish wife, born for dog devotion. Demure, not beautiful but comely enough, an excellent cook, and passionate in cleaning. A bridegroom was picked up for her already, a kosher butcher—but then, pogrom after pogrom, typhoid after typhoid, Revolution followed by the Civil War, the bridegroom was lost somewhere in-between, before she had ever had a chance to see him. Unsullied, Rosa joined the army of proletarians. Her great-cousin Aaron Garlic, having sewn the Superintendent a new sheepskin, spared her the fate of a brigade kitchen maid, so that Rosa went to work straight for Hugh Winter. Of the curly Garlic clan, only Rosa and Aaron survived.

For the dessert of her everyday tidying ménage, Rosa always left the Venetian mirrored medicine case over the bathroom sink. Mr. Winter's shaving apparel caused her special admiration. A yellow and green striped tube of Nennen shaving cream with rich white stuff inside, fat bourgeois she called it lovingly, got thinner and thinner every day until, dystrophic, already a skinny bourgeois, it was replaced by a new, identical tube. Then a black Gillette leather treasury box with a silver-necked razor, kosher butcher she named it, and she talked to them flirtatiously while wiping them of the shaving residue of the morning. The climax of her ritual was a dark turquois flask, golden-friezed, with the number 4711 in the middle. 47, the age of her mother when she had had her last child; 11, the number of Garlic children. Guiltily, Rosa would open the lid—every day she promised herself she wouldn't do it again because Mr. Winter might notice and she would be fired. She drew in the breathtaking perfume, sure it was what Eden smelled like—mellow herbs, wonderful fruit she could not discern—and tilted the bottle neck against her index finger for a spell of a second, inhaling the fragrance from her fingertip as long as it exuded delight, all the way to the bunkhouse she shared with 20 single women of the dam: concrete mixers, dishwashers, wall painters. Even at night she could feel the 4711 under her army blanket.

The very first time the fox-haired boss-shiksa came to Mr. Winter's cottage, his bedroom filled with feral smell. After she left, his suit appeared to be all torn, as well as the blue shirt he was wearing that day. Rosa called Aaron to come to the cottage and mend the suits and the shirts. Later, he was commanded to narrow Winter's clothes, for Mister Hugh had indeed lost some weight in the unpredictability of the Dnieper. Quotidian hydraulic siestas contributed to his weight loss as well. Rosa envied Darya Katz—and hated her guts.

13.

At the outskirts of the construction site, at a maximum possible distance from the worker camp, there squats a spacy bunkhouse with a sign "Torgsin—a Store of Foreign Trade" with merchandise from abroad on display. Only the higher-positioned Soviet staff of the dam and Hugh Winter are allowed to come inside. To buy the cheapest article, a bar of Belgian chocolate, a builder or a digger would have to fork out a week's wages. Two militia guards walk around the bunkhouse, fiddling with their shotguns. The merchandise is not of supreme freshness. To be more exact, it is more or less beyond expiry date.

The shop assistant is Armaïs Esaw-Yantz, an Armenian with the nostrils of a cunning bay mule, all square about him, from head to the tips of his fingers. He leans onto the counter with an expectant air.

"Khow do you like this?"

On the patch of the counter cleared from smoked sausages, sweets, cigars, and Dutch cheese, Armaïs spreads a big sheet of wrapping paper. Onto it, he plunges a heavy roll of cream silk. The bulk of fabric falls with a taut, juicy bang, the same sound Mania produced when swishing out of her mother onto the table back in

Moscow Gunpowder Factory Hospital. A fragile cloud of cream taffeta perches itself upon the silk, like meringues at Darya's fifth birthday; the Snow Queen's blue brocade; a roll of rose-golden thread, with pale intent eyes of pearl buttons gazing at it, in wary array on the cardboard plate. Another, heavier roll thumps down beside the silk: with a tubby flap, charcoal wool of noble strictness, with the North Sea in its fibers.

"Well done, Armaïs," Darya says, checking her facial muscles lest her excitement be revealed, "Now show the shoes."

"Khere," says Armaïs. "Aren't they fit for a kween?"

She can already smell the fine leather from under the greasy counter, the univocal fragrance of the Lanvin store in Paris, Rue du Faubourg Saint-Honoré. ("We are not buying anything this time, we swear," Duchess Senior used to say at the entrance. In an hour, the servants would lug ten, fifteen treasure cartons to the Ritz: whimsical hummer, purple, leopard-patterned leather beauties inside, each pair the price of a good farmhouse. Envious chaperons supported the swooning mother and daughter, both limp in pulse, petted to exhaustion by the shop girls' flattery.)

The first touch with blind fingers inside the half-open carton meets the long-forgotten wonder, calf leather as thin as her own skin; alas, already smoother. The steep hip of the rear, the silk hollow of the insole, the stiff, indomitable column of a heel and a lace ribbon on the front. Darya feels each thrilling knot of the ornament, lingers another moment, then slowly, irrevocably, removes the lid off the carton…

"But I said cream leather, not black, villain!" Ex-Duchess exclaims, enraged.

"Akh, why are you so picky? Loulou said Koko Chanel forbids to wear anything but black this season—they khadn't found kream shoes in the khole of Paris."

"What do you understand in fashion, woodpecker!"

"Khad I stayed in Paris, Duchesse, I would now be designing kostumes for Moulin Rouge—ah my friend Toulouse-Lautrec, khe said, 'Armaïs, you are so fortunate to not khave my kheight.' You name a woman on khis pictures, and I khave known kher—klosely!—too."

"Lautrec died before your first nocturnal emission."

"What a petty, leery pedant of a woman," Esaw-Yantz shakes his head. "Whatever you fancy to think, Madamsel—in this dam dirt, black is the best kolor for shoes."

"Well, then," Darya says, regaining composure, "now take down this: two hazel grouses and a calf's tongue, a bottle of Madeira wine, semi-sweet, sturgeon caviar, pickles, a lobster, Kabul soya sauce, capers, 20 quail eggs, French vinegar, and an ounce of Oil de Provence. The rest of the money I gave you is definitely enough."

"Are you joking with me, your Ekkselency?" asks Armaïs. "Your lousy two thousand were spent long ago. My men with your goods, they were nearly captured and shot in Odessa. The customs, the ship captains to be bribed! My smugglers won't risk their lives for a copeck. They need more if you don't want them to eat your quail eggs on the way khere. And your shoes—my Loulou is the best tart at Moulin Rouge, she khas no idea of the ridikulous Soviet salaries. Do you think my people do all this for the love of your strawberry khair?"

"Esaw-Yantz, don't tell me your Sindbad fairytales. Food is cheaper to get than silk."

"It's Odyssey no less, Komrade Katz. The khungry

Moskow, the dragon laws, Siberia for ten years—it's better to be shot dead on place."

"I don't have more and you know it damn well. A thousand has been bursting enough, even if I asked for an ermine pelisse besides. Don't lie to me, Esaw-Yantz, you are not going to pay your cutthroats more."

"Think as you please, but mind you: I kan write elokwent delations in Russian. I will besing you in them, and I know kho will love to read them—those tough men will be moved to tears!"

It's not that Darya Katz looks forward to the rest of her life all that much. Nor that she couldn't blackmail Armaïs Esaw-Yantz with his file, filled with the grout of all calibers, from misdemeanors to felonies. It is just a pity to clip the wings of her venture in mid-flight.

"I don't have any more money, Armaïs," she repeats softly.

"In this kase, your Ex-Ekksellency, there is one way to pay. Not much of kondescension on your part, mind you, I khail from Armenian counts myself."

"Your otherwise loud file is suspiciously silent about it," Darya remarks.

Esaw-Yantz takes her by the shoulder, turning her in the direction of the storeroom.

"Finish the list first," says Darya, pushing his square hand away.

"Anchovy, capers, quail eggs, Kabul soya sauce. Sturgeon caviar; red caviar, five pounds, Massandra, five bottles from Tsar's wine reserves. You will not get Queen of Hawaii, my favorite, cuvee of 1891, but cuvee 1905, Grapes of Wrath, might still be left."

"Goody-good," says Armaïs, putting down the pencil,

with a wet smile, "I kan swear by my two sons you will khave fun."

14.

Petro unloads the burlap sack, heavy as lead, at the storehouse stoop. He was ordered to transport it on a donkey cart all the way from Torgsin. He was told those were new blankets for the workers for the coming winter, but something shiny pierces the burlap. Petro ascribes it to hangover shimmering in his eyes.

"Now go fool, go to work," Darya urges Petro.

Aaron hauls the sack further into his den. Disguised under a couple of blankets is a tailor's dream. Aaron sniffs the silk, the taffeta, the wool, and bursts into tears.

Guard of hoes, robes, blankets, sheets, burlap sacks, simple medicine, Aaron misses his vocation so much: he used to be the best tailor in Zaporozhye. All the nobility had their clothes sewn by him. He was the famous specialist for crinoline. Whether the Marshal, his wife or mistresses, or the Town Mayor, or the merchants' wives—only Aaron Garlic was trusted to do the best job.

Aaron is squiggly and infinitesimally small like all men of his lineage, almost a dwarf, with sharp features making him look more like blackamoor than a Jew. An age-long ghetto gossip had it that the great Russian poet Alexander Sergeyevich Pushkin had stayed in his grandfather's inn, receiving too much attention from his grandmother, but as Aaron loved to say dismissingly, "And King Solomon also stayed at my grandfather's inn, in all his golden attire."

Tailor Garlic spoke Russian in blank verse, sometimes simian-rhymed, his phrases tiding, ebbing, keeping the customers under the spell of his parlance. "I'll take you into Onion Sealand, with silk as sweet as marzipan," he would sibilate in a mesmerizing whisper. Chalk behind his ear, tailor's meter creeping all around like viper, rich ladies never noticed how Aaron came to measuring their deep internal parameters.

With male clients, he sported a jocular, friendly manner that would never let on his behavior with ladies. Not in the most secret intimations, with knees trembling under the embroidery hoops, behind the closed parlor doors, into the petals of whatever roses or lilies they were guiltily growing on canvas, could the renowned wives and maidens afford to even hint that they had been lured into intimacy with a Jewish tailor.

"Your sewing machine will be brought to the warehouse tomorrow. You will work at nights," Darya Katz ordered.

"I have two small children, Dod and Sheila," says Aaron, "and my wife Shoora, she is so devilishly jealous, she will make a Shakespeare tragedie out of my absence."

"I'll give you a paper that ascertains you are working at a task of state dam importance, sewing new bedclothes for the diggers' camp. And this here is your real task," says Ex-Duchess, producing an old photograph, at which Aaron gasps in awe: a full-length portrait of the late Empress, Alexandra Fyodorovna, in an evening gown with a train.

"It was blue with golden embroidery on the hem. She wore it at the last Christmas Ball at the Winter Palace."

Garlic's hands hover about Darya's gaunt body, in love of his trade, in honor of femininity. Bust 28, waist 23, sleeve 32. This woman looks as if born by a sickle moon.

"You should eat more, Your Exceillency, to justify the breast darts."

He kneels and rips up the feeble threads of her underpants middle seam, hips 28.

"I haven't ordered you pants," said Darya, entangled in the creepers of the tailor meter.

"Don't sei so, never sei so, your Exceillency," Aaron replies, very earnestly, "there's a secret measurement I got patented—it's called caper allowance."

The Singer sewing machine clattered its teeth in November cold. In old times, each piece of Garlic clothing was either a poem or a fairy-tale. The Empress' ball dress, however, took a whole saga to sew, eons longer than the usual three fittings. Aaron had prided himself in never needing more than those three thread-needle dates of surging, flourishing, and rounding up. The ladies left the atelier elegant, beautiful, but irreparably dissatisfied with their husbands' love skills.

In the course of Empress' dress revival, Darya found out more about the delicate art of sewing than she had when all taffeta in St. Petersburg could be hers: the all-caressed corset, the sub-crinoline waltz. Strange to say, she found out more about the domain she had prided herself in being a connoisseur of. For the first time, she experienced pure adoration, practically applied.

Each appointment revealed tiny cake-poems of desire, generous and not asking anything in return—and always swathed in a tailor's meter. They were not even personal—Aaron Garlic seemed to be perfectly able to make love to a milkmaid or a concrete layeress in the same manner, but it was impossible to be offended.

Part of nobility's upbringing having been needlework, Darya used to be good at embroidering, especially in fine broderie anglaise. With only a little loving Garlic guidance, she studded the hem of the dress and the train with a bizarre mix of Celtic and oriental silk snake-twists.

"My father was very lean," Darya confided into the embroidery hoop, Aaron's Singer sewing machine a-chatter. "This is why he was so glad when His Majesty announced a costume ball so he could have a boyar prince pelisse sewn, heel-length. Otherwise, the ball protocol prescribed male courtiers to wear knee-length pantaloons. Men's calves had to be of a harmonious form, too fat or too thin were strictly forbidden. So Father always had to wear custom-made stockings padded with cotton wool—false calves. They would always slip sideways, and Dad had to wriggle them on place—oh how the court bitches giggled and whispered."

"Your father didn't know of my patented false calves. Upon my honor, they would never slide," said Aaron, patting Darya on her red curls.

For the time of dressmaking, Brett and her disgraceful behavior stopped bothering the ex-Duchess: Spanish summer, Mikes, Cohns, a torero who had but two women before her. She didn't resent the pug loyalty of her neuter love Jake anymore.

The Winona cottage saw less and less of Darya Katz, and the Simmons bed experienced less and less hydraulics. In early December, she only came for a hot bath and left the best engineer of dams with a Sun that Rose in Vain.

15.

With 20 thousand workers at the Dam now, it is next to impossible to find the culprits of the breakdown. The fall of a rabbet fence at the right bank of the Dnieper cost Haim Katz 50 new gray hairs. It cost Engineer Alexandrov dismissal and arrest on suspicion in connections with international terrorism because he had been seen near the fence at midnight. Also, there were rumors of sabotage.

As Head of Personnel Department, Darya Katz was ordered to deduce who the saboteurs might be, so she just went to the bunkhouses with militia guards and randomly picked out six men for arresting whose appearance was the scruffiest.

It was found out that the metal reinforcing ropes of the fence had been plucked out of the structure and stolen. Thanks to militia's patented methods, the suspects confessed very soon. The Head of Personnel sent them to the tribunal, and the execution followed, instructively illuminated in the Soviet press under the name of "The Vermin of Sabotage" from The Pravda to the The Dam Leaflet. The rabbet fence was restored in a frenzied three days' time.

Not even Engineer Alexandrov, who had indeed, as he had claimed, gone out for a nightly smoke on the right bank, noticed the nimble gypsy brigade at the ignominious rabbet fence, with apelike velocity screwing out bolts, plucking out metal reinforcing ropes. Rom Román and his dun gang were moving as if in other sound frequencies, and with a swiftness unperceivable to the eye.

For catching four foxes quick, a hunter needs 30 traps. It takes a good deal of metal to make 30 gaping grins with clicking tongues for the red beasts to step on. The trap lips should be thin, delicate enough, lest the animal's bones break.

Old blacksmith Rom Stepán melted the metal ropes and the bolts in the furnace he had made of an old oil drum. Horse shoes used to be the top of his mastery, but new times demand new skills, so his bony chest is twinkling with dark nipples in bony wrinkles, in rich sauce of sweat, despite the first snow powdering the brow of the bullock cart.

The Roma boys clubbed a stray mongrel, and the young Aza roasted it on open fire for fox lure. She moved the dog aside, heated water in the camp cauldron, put all the 30 glistening trap grins into it, and spiced the metal broth richly with sagebrush and woodruff. Aza simmered the brew till dawn to efface all traces of human odor from the traps. She sat on Rom Román's lap all night. Clockwise, counterclockwise, fainting and resurrecting in the kind steam, they relished in the distilled heart of the steppe, their profiles sharpened in tension, then languor-blurred.

At gray empty midday, the construction site across the Dnieper was in the main focus of the world: the bulging, the erecting, the mallet clamor, concrete kneaded with renewed, sabotage-purged vigor.

"My Zap in the steppes, Stronghold of the country, On muscles and blood, On the verve of new times," Darya's song resounded from the right bank to the left.

The gypsy band swept along the river on tiptoe, dragging the roasted dog along the fox track. They carried the traps on long wooden spades, to preserve the fresh steppe breath of the iron jaws. The Roma discharged the traps carefully off the spades, under the nightly fox trails on thin snow, into the moldering salad of fallen leaves.

16.

The first snow ensnared the river Dnieper in dark gray attire. Considerably shrunk in height but glossing with surfeit, Glutton Rapid plunged into winter hibernation.

"Ah, Nikolai, I can't believe Bitch Katz gave us a whole day off, and a whole sausage, isn't she nice!"

"Did you see how Bitch Katz leered at me when giving us the medal? As if she wanted to eat me up alive."

"Yes, yes, what did she say, for your ingenitality," said the proud Petro, patting his medal, on which the words "Valiant Soviet Laborer" were engraved.

"Ingenuity, fool, ingenuity, as if you deserved a reward!"

"But it had been all my idea to fill the hole with ice."

"Idea up your arse!"

The sun travels its low November itinerary all too fast. The sausage is eaten up, the bottle of vodka finished, but the whole day off brought no result whatsoever in treasure finding. Thin stars are rare and sleepy in the sky.

"Maybe it's neither a willow nor a lime but an oak?—we've never looked under oaks," ventures Petro—"if our granddads drank as much as we do it's no wonder they could have mixed up the tree names."

"Look at this smart prick. He dares to question family

truths! Well, let's check, and if we don't find anything under yonder oak overlooking the Glutton—woe to you."

Under the oak, there lies a massive stone, all overgrown with moss.

"See the stone? Just as my dad said," Petro is excited.

Nikolai scrapes some moss off with his fingernails, and sees cuneiform-like letters wedged into the stone, like Braille. It is too dark to make anything out, but this is a sure sign.

"Goody-good, fat fart, your luck is with you, for now!" Nikolai grins.

Petro smiles triumphantly. He sinks his shovel under the mighty tree. The ground is hard and dry but very soon, the spade reaches a cloth—the prize is definitely near. It must be the beginning of an unraveling garment, a wrapping of something precious. Here, a gold coin is already glistening. Petro stoops to pick it up, but the golden thing does not come off—it is a sewed-on button.

"Stop digging, idiot, here is a dead man's arm!" Nikolai recoils.

"Pax, pax, Holy Mother of God!" Petro chokes, "We must've hit some mass grave."

During the Civil war, there was no time to bury the dead deep. Two foot was the average in executioners' patience.

"He was a Cossack! Here, the uniform, a kaftan, a peaked cap! No-no, this is a bad sign, a curse, leave it now. Why have I listened to you again," cries Nikolai. He aims at Petro's back with his shovel, "Was it this we came all the way here for?"

Petro rebounds, shrieking in a very unmale manner, as if the dead Cossack clenched him by the foot, wanting to pull him down into the soil. But it is a glistening fox trap

Petro is caught in. He tries to cast the thing off but the metal grin clenches its teeth ever harder.

"Serve you right, the curse has already worked on you," says Nikolai. "I'm going to the barracks to fetch a clipper to free you, clumsy bastard."

"Don't leave me here, it's spooky at the grave edge," implores Petro, but Nikolai speeds up for the digger camp. He has no slightest intention to return—is he stupid to ramble to and fro through the dark, half an hour walk one way? He is through with the treasure hunt, his own gourd dearer to him. Now, at this short hour of night, he must take his advantage of being up while all the other diggers are fast asleep: cookie Masha will belong to him alone.

"Ai-ne-ne-ne," laughed Rom Román, "This is not a fox but a whole fat, bald bear." He released the trap grip and freed the fainted Petro, surprisingly alive. His foot turned into a cocktail of boot leather, bones and sinews. Román tore off a strap off his dingy shirt and bandaged the digger's wound.

"You wicked gypsy, I'll complain to the Superintendent," Petro gnarled.

"Go on," said Rom Román, nonchalant. This was the last trap check, and he needed no more foxes. Three had died in the traps overnight, in unequal fight with the humid cold and the portage chain. On a path overlooking One Too Much Rapid, he approached the last deadly sickle, embracing the fourth, motionless beast. But as soon as Rom Román took the red carcass by the scruff to throw into the sack, its black bead eyes opened, the muzzle swung back and thrust its sharp teeth deep into Román's wrist.

"Always better off, scoundrel," said Nikolai at Petro's

bed, pouring him out some moonshine: Petro was firmly stuck in the infirmary with amputated toes and pneumonia.

"I wish that trap had caught me—then I would be wallowing around in the warm bed like a tom-cat in butter and not drudge away in this dam cold."

"Why didn't you come back? I nearly bled to death, froze my balls off."

"I already took a clipper and went out, but Shitpick was prowling around the camp like a jackal with a gun," Nikolai lied. "You would have lost your best friend."

17.

Seven files on the Head of Personnel's desk, the winners of her private competition. Before the revolution, she would have had a lean chance to encounter these people, let alone get involved in a communication of any intense kind. Alas, they were the only surviving remnants of the old epoch, thin milk of toppled times instead of the vanished cream.

Feldsher Boris Mandarinov, former spa doctor. Welder Gleb Eelovy, five semesters at Oxford University, never graduated. Bricklayer Vassili Bogomole, once Deacon of Kherson Candlemas Cathedral. Plumber Semén Ticklick, before the revolution, Warrant Officer in Tsar's private Guard Squad. Field cook Matvey Porko, a former chef.

Digger Nikolai Peasdick, of Cossack descent. Darya looked up Nikolai's file, that Slavic Rudolf Valentino: no military title, hadn't even been a cornet or a corporal—the origins too base, not much different from a moujik. Anyway, morning sickness left her no space for any risqué desires. She sighed and shoved Nikolai's file back into the ever-filling, ever more bursting cabinet—60 thousand workers on the construction site by now.

Darya's menstrual cycle had always been ragtime, so

she did not notice a quarter rest turn into a half, and then a whole that stretched into a longa. She decided to conceal her pregnancy as long as possible: there was still so much to do. She tied some sage brush into a little handkerchief to ward off the hellish dam rainbow of welded iron, kneaded concrete, workers' sweat, and a stew of feces and chlorine.

The Soviet industry now has no time for petty frills—anything less than a lathe or a turbine is petty, not worth attention, but a resemblance of happy New-Year expectance must be induced among the dam people—to chase them unto ever higher peaks of labor achievement, to divert their thoughts from the paltry wages. So the Head of Propaganda announced a competition for the best self-made toy for the plump New Dam Year tree placed in the infirmary, "for our ailing brothers in dam labor," in unequal combat with broken bones, typhus, pneumonia, dysentery, or consumption.

Decorations in the old regime style were disqualified at once. Darya expressed Dam contempt to angels in cotton wool clouds. Little tin crowns, unimaginative pine cones and acorns wrapped in aluminum foil were labeled as ugly démodé. Any toys representing food, especially fat-dotted sausage or chicken legs, were condemned as gluttony-bourgeois. Darya fined any dam employee who submitted such artifacts by confiscation of a day's ratio food card.

As Dam-decent samples were declared: red stars, mini guns, hand-grenades—or, in a worker-peasant key, proletarian tools like spades, rakes, hammers, sickles and tiny wrenches, all cast in self-made molds on fire or primus stoves. Regardless of their artistic value, all of them went onto the New Dam Year tree. Stooping, sweating and swearing, the ailing brothers in labor decorated the beautiful, opulent pine tree, for installing which two infirmary bunk beds had to be removed—an ironworker's, whose dysentery was not all that bad, and Petro's, whose good leg was strong enough to hobble on.

Darya carefully chose the winner with a pedagogical aim: female, and not a notable concrete layeress or welderess at that.

"The smallest assistants to our great cause can also display wonders of proletarian talent and should be well respected for their merits Dam-wide," she announced at the morning assembly. The winning toy was carried along the first two front rows of the personnel by a militia guard: it was a Red Army soldier made with obvious love, a beaked woolen helmet on its tin crown, with a five-finger red star sewn up upon it, and a smart duffle coat.

Blushed cookie Masha stepped forward to receive her award, a book entitled "The Dignity of a Soviet Woman, or Procreation Is Only Possible in Soviet Marriage." Darya cast a muting look at the diggers who were unanimously giggling into their sleeves. In her nausea, Head of Propaganda overlooked the simple personnel file fact that Masha was illiterate. Moreover, there had been no way to divine that, even if read aloud, cookie Masha would not have been able to benefit from the book. She had already been brigade-impregnated, approximately at the same time with Darya herself.

18.

On the clothes line behind the Winona cottage, the moon outlines Hugh Winter's laundered outfit, the limp linen ghosts smelling freshly of soap and frost. None of the gypsy men possesses a robust pair of pants: the clan is too impoverished after the revolution, having lost all the rich customers who used to buy horses, listen to singing or have their fate foretold. The Roma only have the clothes they wear—remaining naked when they wash it. The necklaces of 20-dollar American coins that once tinkled on their women's necks dissolved, coin by coin, along the errant lines of the camp's Europe-long itinerary. The golden Austrian ducats sewed up to their blouses and shawls were all long ago ripped out by the militia squads—swapped for freedom. Men's chests house wind and snow, their leg hairs peep through the thin tatters of what were once called pants.

Rom Román has already scraped the fat off the fox hides, broken the fox skulls, and taken out the pink brains, with which he greased the pelts. He softened the beasts over the stake till they became docile. Now he needs two tough pairs of pants for smoking the hides.

There is a pair of gray wool slacks on the clothes line:

too elegant, it would be scorched by the smoke if used. But next on the rope is a whole fortress of pants: two dark blue identical twins, of stiff cotton cloth one could make a tent of. The stitching is unusually outside, running a-shimmer in a tireless dotted trail along the seams. Two back pockets, a crotch rivet, a chinchback, and a fly of six silver buttons. On the belt patch, a word of five Latin letters, and number 201. If only his Roma could be equipped with such pants! Then they would never freeze. But only the rich men like this American could afford such clothing. Román unpins the stiff blue pants and carries them, like logs under his armpit, to the Caucasus camp.

The piece of string goes from the beasts' eyeholes to an overhead tree branch. He sews the bottom of each hide to each pant leg and covers a pot with the cinchback pant bum. He gazes at the drooping tails. In two hours, the pelts acquire a nice tan as if kissed by the Crimean sun. Rom Román undoes the pelts and puts on the pleasantly warm steaming pants, the same color as the night sky, the fly buttons like stars. He strokes the red pelts as if they were dogs.

One red beast in his hand, he steps into Aza's family tent. Her father, blacksmith Stepán, snores in the far corner. Aza is sniffing sweetly to the left of the entrance on a huge down pillow, bestrewn by her younger siblings. The only fat shapes in the camp are pillows. They are dearer than gold, warmth being the main currency of gypsy winter, a warrant of procreation and the best dowry, now that horses are scarce and gaunt. Rom Román shakes the snotty minnow off the pillow. The red pelt skulks unhurriedly along the girl's body, circling

around, resting in each nook and cranny, two days ago a
wary predator, now a tool of love.

19.

"Curved Poo?" Rosa asks again, and giggles against her will.

"No, it's krumkake. "Káke" is cake in Norwegian," explains Hugh Winter solemnly.

"Drei Eier," he says, pointing at the eggs in the fridge—"Drey ey," Rosa repeats diligently.

Half kubok tsuker, half kubok puter, eyn kubok mel, eyn kubok krem, vanille, kardamon, registers Rosa, her listening comprehension skills honed by adoration. She remembers Hugh giving her a sum of her week's wages and sending her to Torgsin, just for vanilla and cardamom, which Armaïs produced from under the counter with a saucy wink, then an ambiguous touch of his hand on hers—she left the shop hastily, blushing beetroot-red.

Although religion is the opium, the enemy of the people, Iosif Viscerionovich Stalin ordered for the best American engineer to not be deprived of his usual holidays. Hugh Winter is allowed to celebrate his capitalist Christmas on December 24th.

Mr. Winter is not at work. He sits in the hot bath for a long time with the Hemingway Darya returned at last—the book is too European for his taste, too Bohemian, the people in it seem to always drink and never to work. Hugh puts on a bath robe and about 6:00 PM changes into his best suit. He shaves, sprays himself with a double portion of 4711 eau de cologne and enters the dining room of the "Winona."

The flushing piles of baked filigree cones, their ornaments repeating the frost lace of the cottage windows, sticking out the playful tongues of whipped cream—Hugh Winter is moved. The waffles came out exact and immaculate, like his dam drafts translated into the language of dessert. The young woman is trying to interpret his countenance, moving her lips as if reading in whisper.

At the back of her head, gratitude to Mister Winter still flickers, for not accusing her of the disappearance of the tough blue working pants. He took it easily, believing in her total integrity. He knew who it was once he saw a gypsy man pass by, wearing unmistakably them, but soot-black and burnt on the cuffs (Attn. Superintendent Katz: Herewith I bring to your awareness the theft and mutilation of two pairs of my blue denim jeans, Levi's 201 brand, the cost of which was $20.00 apiece. The gypsy band is to blame. I demand urgent measures—Hugh Winter).

The renowned American engineer wipes his hands on a napkin, sprawls his fingers fan-like, and enters the hidden black forest of hair under Rosa's kerchief. Holding her nape, he draws her face to him. He steers the heavy abundance, the Siamese trinity of lips, breasts and hips, towards the dining room arch, to the Simmons bed in graceline tubing. The soft streaks of cardamom reach as far as the bedroom, a whiff of vanilla is on the pillow and under the moving blanket, Rosa's body itself sweet dough where Hugh is enmeshed like nuts and raisins.

"R-r-rose," American whisper rustles into the small pink ear, from now on the ear of a personal Zap field wife of the best engineer of dams.

On the New Year's Eve, Darya stopped by at the Winona for the last time. Winter greeted her with a benevolent, non-committal air of an overfed tom-cat, which was not at all his typical behavior in her presence. The beetle she-thing was busy about the house, strangely a-blush, a little slower than usual, and somehow more dignified.

"Why are you not in your barrack at this curfew time of the evening?" Darya asked strictly, "the dam does not pay for unqualified overtime work."

Rosa lowered her head, clutching the handle of a saucepan.

"I've given her some cooking to do. She loves cooking more than life," Hugh said.

"Take care she doesn't bake someone's rooster in her oven, for there is also a way to roast her."

This was a case for a duchess to leave with indignation, but it was not what the nauseous Comrade Katz could now afford.

"Your Christmas is over, Hugh," she said, containing herself, "how about borrowing me the Victrola with your glorious records?"

"This is a very valuable thing, Darr—" Hugh started.

"As if I didn't know! My job requires me to get the ailing Soviet hero construction workers acquainted with your American proletarian music. They will adore your collection. Don't you love our indigenous folk, don't you want to help them? Can't tell a monkey from a wrench, but what wits, what power of spirit—didn't you say that yourself?"

The argument was more than weighty, Hugh had but to agree. The heavers came and transported the walnut cupboard to the Infirmary. Hugh Winter sat down at his desk.

> Attn. Superintendent Katz: Herewith I am expressing my deepest satisfaction with the excellent work of my housemaid Rosa Garlic. I will adamantly protest any attempts to replace her, in which case I shall untimely leave the construction site.

In his fifth Dnieper year, the best engineer of dams grasped the local hydraulics of having one's way. He made Rosa the necessary prerequisite of his well-being at the dam, and his well-being was ordained by Iosif Viscerionovich Stalin himself. Hugh suspected, had he ordered a harem of concubines on camelbacks, they would have been delivered to the Winona without much delay.

The sick workers listened to "The Moonlight," and "The Bear's Oil," and then one patient said in a thin voice, "Comrade Head of Propaganda, don't you have our Russian Kalinka for us? What you put on is foreign bullshit."

"Better bring us some vodka and fuck whatever music," said another ailing comrade.

On the sixth of January, all the infirmary patients were sent to their barracks for a leave. The building had, ostensibly, to be sanitized.

20.

"Look, the tit of a negress! And a golden mouth on top, it can suck you in!"

"Have you ever seen a real negress, moron?"

"Why, on pictures of the African proletariat, in The Pravda! They always wear their tits bare."

"Even so, how can a negress' nipple be as pink as a Ukrainian broad's? And have you never seen a gramophone record, fool?"

Nikolai and Petro, the heroes of the dam, felt they deserved a bottle of spirits for Ex-Christmas. They knocked at the infirmary door, but no one opened. Petro put his nose against the frost-chained window and breathed like a locomotive. He looked through the cleared patch of glass.

"Look, Cook Porko! Who is he grabbing?"

"It's our boss bitch, dressed up like a fucking tsarina! She looked at me and she looked at me, and I thought she would ask me for a fuck me, but no, she didn't even invite me to her party."

"Here's Gleb Eelovy, too, in a tailcoat, skinny ape—I saw him drinking dehorn yesterday! And he is there, but I'm not."

One after another, the discs rotate under the needle in a tireless fouetté of their black tutus, their waists lavender, purple, scarlet, ochre. The beds are propped against the walls, in two, three stories, to make space for the party activities. In the middle of the room, there is the New Year tree, now called the Christmas pine.

In the scrub room, Aaron Garlic poured the finished ball dress upon Darya like cream-golden rain, matched the breast darts with breasts, noting their recent fullness. Clasp by clasp, he fastened the blue brocade corset on her back. Darya was shivering, and Aaron clouded her neck and shoulders in a fox boa he had sewn out of the Roma-tanned fox hides. The boa warmed her instantly, but she had to contain an insistent call of nausea at the clash of the streaming silk fragrance and the terse note of smoke spiced with a tepid hint of carrion. The hides had smelled much worse when Román cast them on her stoop at dawn—of an insanitary gypsy tent and a nomad woman's lap. Aaron Garlic did his best to deodorize the fur, but whenever a woman gets in the way of Head of Personnel, be it unawares, there are grave consequences to face.

Aaron had turned the leftover pieces of silk, taffeta, brocade and golden thread into clouds, snowflakes, and the very anti-Soviet angels that had been strictly discarded at the Dam New Year toy competition. Blue-bodied, winged puppets dangle from the low ceiling, leaping up from the dancers' movements. Late Empress Alexandra Fyodorovna shakes finely on a bedside table, trying to abandon the frames of the photograph, to restore justice, to outshine her dress-twin impostrix.

"Please my Duchess, I'm pleading you to understand I must disappear from the dam tonight—my wife thinks

I'm involved in some anti-Soviet plot and is deeply worried I will be arrested."

Aaron looks tender, guilty, and weak—weak, which made it easy for Darya to discard him like a toy she had outgrown.

"The Moor has done his duty, the moor needn't escape through the back door," she said coldly, "Here's a legal dam-leaving permit, God speed."

Aaron bowed, in a nimble, almost ball-appropriate way, and sped away on his trochee feet.

Ex-Duchess charcoals her eyelashes and applies a stub of an ancient French rouge on her lips. Her ears can boast no pearls, her fingers no diamonds to shimmer in candlelight, but the dress is a ball statement enough.

The six invited men appeared in Garlic-tailored tailcoats. Since new shoes for them had not been on Armaïs Esaw-Yantz's supply list, they are shyly hiding their boots, albeit wiped and blacked to the utmost degree, but gaping with opened seams, mangled by five dam winters and many a dirt track. The men are self-conscious of each other, too.

"Today I'm not Comrade Katz for you, gentlemen," Darya announces. "Call me Duchess, which, deep inside, I have never ceased to be. Dance and entertain me with stories of a life bygone, a life to be conjured up only now, and maybe, only once."

Cook Porko uncorks the first bottle of Grapes of Wrath. The Victrola is playing a pink labeled record, Chopin, a polonaise in A-flat major. Darya sieves through men's hands half-swooning, and her dance steps falter a bit. It would have been impossible to structure the ball as it was appropriate, and she knew she would have to bear the crackling of the record instead of a live orchestra;

still, perfection was worth to strive at. For each item of real music, Darya paid Armaïs a special sex service he had pre-ordered. Backwards meringue for the Strauss, straddle split galore for the Strauss, the price of each further record unutterable without a shudder. The stunts were so difficult to perform against the throbbing background of sickness.

"I know I'm not invited, but even if you fell on your knees out of your own accord," Armaïs said, putting on his pants, and biscuited me French style better than Loulou kherself, even then wouldn't I go to your party. You will pay dearly for your stunt, but I, I must live on and witness my sons bekome famous, and I must khelp them with the little money I khave made on you: my elder boy will be a doktor, the most wanted, best doktor—khe will live in doktor paradise, only pussy, pussy, all day long. And my younger boy, oh, khe will be an Armenian Toulouse-Lautrec, but handsome, like me, and as tall as my unfulfilled dream."

The ball was in no way impromptu. The future guests were summoned to her office on the six days preceding the event, separately, under the pretext of interrogation as to their current political reliability, regarding their non-proletarian descent. Under the threat of arrest, they were instructed not to tell anyone of the dance lining of the interrogation. To garnish the appointment with truth, she wrote a patriotic stanza for each of the barracks the men came from, and told them to teach these verses to their bunkhouse mates, which was duly checked at the Morning Dam Assembly.

Cook Porko's three fingers clutch Darya's wrist while she wraps him up in Haydn's minuet. His right little and ring fingers were caught in the electric mincer at the onset of his dam cook career and served to some unaware worker for lunch meatballs.

The Olivier salad was on the main menu list of Amerika Restaurant. Yes, they say it was the great poet Pushkin's favorite treat. Back then, Chef Porko was not particularly impressed by the dish, but now he deliberately left his hands unwashed to preserve the enjoyment of his suddenly resuscitated chef past. The ingredients arrived to the backyard of the kitchen-factory in an ice crate: two hazel grouses and a calf's tongue, a bottle of Madeira wine, semi-sweet, sturgeon caviar, pickles, a lobster, Kabul soya sauce, capers, 20 quail eggs, French vinegar and an ounce of Oil de Provence.

On the kerosene stove brought to the infirmary from home, Matvey roasted the grouses golden and simmered them in Madeira. He boiled the calf tongue and the speckled pearly eggs, then sliced the pickles and arranged everything on three aluminum plates. A delightful feeling to be cooking manually again, with first-rate products, after shameful years of pulling the kitchen-factory levers, of trying not to inhale the odors of hellish brews called food.

Pubescent double basses trample the honey blond violins, and the chef's boot rebounds on Darya's black shoe.

"Mind your rhythm, Mister Porko, one-two-three," says Ex-Duchess, containing a shriek.

She throws a handkerchief of cream silk snippets, to Feldsher Boris Mandarinov. During the rehearsals, the ex-spa doctor proved to be much more nimble in his limbs, so he could be entrusted with Tchaikovsky's "Waltz of Snowflakes."

Eye to eye with the tall Head of Propaganda, his thumb

and middle finger almost meeting around her waist, Doctor Mandarinov could examine her anemic texture, sluggish circulation, dark circles under her eyes—kidney malfunction, the pulse of her filigree wrist disjointed; just a doctor's hunch—possible pregnancy, of about 12 weeks. Still, this woman is a dazzling species: sad mermaid irises, her décolleté a March glade, cross-stitched with subcutaneous blue streams.

"I would kidnap you, Excellency, to Sochi in Indian summer—the lazy sea sunsets, the shadows of palm-trees. I'd feed you with pomegranates and delight you with iodine waters. We'd glide in sulphide healing muds smoother than this waltz and wash ourselves in the sea," he whispers boldly in French. I would give you a directed Vichy shower, scald-chill, scald-chill, to summon pink to your cheeks."

Pectoral violas bring forth crystal triangles, and a choir sweeps a silver snowstorm upon the royal dress.

The outside gapers clear a bigger patch in the infirmary glass with their breath. They trample a gray island in the snow.

"See how he grabs her? It could have been me, but I wouldn't have been such a pantywaist, I'd have shown her the hardcore," Nikolai hits his palms against each other, trying to light a roll-up.

Even fitted by Aaron's deft hand, the tailcoat still hangs about the ex-eternal student of Philosophy Gleb Eelovy. Strauss Jr.'s sturdy "Odeon Quadrille" almost blows the grasshopper of a man off his feet.

"When at Oxford, Your Excellency," he says with almost King's English pronunciation (which was the main reason for his invitation), "oh, how I argued with Professor Lewis Carroll! I pointed out six logical mistakes in his

Alice— may I list them for you. First— while rose-dyeing –"

"Lewis Carroll died eight years before you learned to say 'mama,'" Darya remarks.

"But by and by," Eelovy was not discouraged by Darya's truthful statement in the least, "Mr. Carroll recognized my superiority, and he was beaten, shattered by my perspicacity! His stutter got even worse. This was why he did his best to expel me from Oxford: my intellect was all too much for him to endure."

Darya ended his sentence with an exclamation mark of her heel on his shoe.

"You were thrown out for debauchery."

To Bach's "Sarabande D minor," Vassili Bogomole leads Darya through the room in his elephantine pace, her black-clod feet in constant danger of getting squashed into pulp.

"It is a wee bit eerie, Your Excellency, that holy icons are missing in this Christmas of ours," Ex-Deacon begins cautiously.

"Possessing items of religious cult equals ten years of exile—mind your rhythm, Deacon."

"I would have painted one just for this Holy Night if you had said a word—what a painter I used to be! On the right chapel of my Kherson Cathedral, I painted Doomsday with so horrid a devil that babies burst into tears from the first look."

"For me, Christmas has always been a prop, an excuse to highlight myself. And for you it is a primitive reflex you've just been deprived of for too long. You have come here tonight even knowing you'd have to besmirch yourself with secular dancing."

This Head of Propaganda woman, Ex-Deacon finds,

resembles a sore Whore of Babylon, but the degree of her sadness, the pitch of her fall, is not to tell. Strangely enough, her ever-prodding husband makes an exception to Vassili, never coming nearer, never finding fault with his work, and always looking away when he is near. Bogomole has an impression that they met before, probably many years ago, but he can't remember where and under what circumstances.

Saint-Saëns, ideal for crowning the ball with his nimble Danse Macabre—Darya'd better not remember what Esaw-Yantz had charged for it.

"You need a private bodyguard," says Tsar's ex-Warrant Officer Semén Ticklick. This duchess is as fragile as cigarette tissue. She looks like a spitting image of a very expensive cocotte he could never afford at Madame Coucou's, not with his salary back in St. Petersburg. Now, although he would never dare to even touch her in a sensuous way, here she is, in his arms, albeit for a dance. He tries to compliment her appearance in neandertal French, but she gags his mouth with a reeking fox tail.

Darya feels she is being led by a mechanically dancing skeleton: no litheness of flesh in ex-Warrant Officer, and Ticklick's grip is too tight.

"I became the private diary watchman of His Majesty, I know all the mistresses he had, and all perverse thoughts—he himself told me all about it at a glass of champagne."

"His Majesty never committed adultery, and he didn't like champagne, and you never saw Him closer than from 100 feet distance. You were in the common guard squadron."

The oboe cockerel crows the end of the dance, and she pushes him away with a light, final pizzicato.

At recess, the guests go to the operation table for the only available food, the genuine Olivier salad served on canteen plates with pewter cutlery.

"Gentlemen—you tried as best you could," says Ex-Duchess, "and all of you will be rewarded. Bogomole, you will become our new stock clerk and Dam painter—no, don't flatter yourself, you have no talent, but what you can smear will be enough for Dam purposes—my God, to think that Nicholas Roerich portrayed me once… anyway, I hope you'll make anyone you depict look a freak enough."

"God bless your slave Darya," said Vassili Bogomole softly.

"Porko, you are appointed Chief Chef of the Dam canteen. Eelovy, Ticklick, you have no better qualification to boast of than adamant lying. I can't think of any promotion, but I'm kindly increasing your salary by three rubles a month. Mandarinov—you ascend from feldsher to Dam Doctor; for inappropriate innuendos, no salary increase," at which words the infirmary clock strikes midnight. Unanimously, the guests bow to the ground. It is not to tell what they think of Darya's benefaction.

Befuddled, full of contained flatulence, they sing the state hymn, not of the "Union of So-o-viet Uni-i-ted Republics" but the old one of the Russian Empire, "Lord, Guard our Tsar."

"Who hung this disgrace on the Christmas tree?" Darya Katz suddenly inquires, tearing a toy off a fir branch. She flings the window leaf open. In breaks the icy air, out swishes a tin Red Army soldier in its beaked helmet and duffle coat. The guests applaud. The tin soldier hits Petro right on his pate.

"To Your Dam Majesty," toasts the spa doctor Mandarinov, genuflect, and kisses Darya's hand.

"To Our Dam Majesty!" echo the other men, and, for a spell, Darya's nausea subsides.

"Bitch along, bitch across!" gasps Nikolai with his nose firmly stuck to the window glass, "this is high treason no less!"

"Fuck-a-bye twice! Let's tell the barrack blokes what we've seen. This story's worth five vodka bottles!" raves Petro, icicles under his nostrils.

"No, you dung heap, we'll be dead silent about it until it comes in handy," says Nikolai, "and don't limp as if overrun by a train. It was just a lousy fox trap."

21.

"It is not my job to accompany you there at my wife's whim," said vexed Katz. "Why have you come to bother me at this late hour, the whole squad of you?"

He was hoping for a quiet night—Christmas, whether Western or Orthodox, had never been on his biographical agenda. Not even after getting baptized would he remember the date, now that all religion was forbidden.

"Who is Superintendent here, I wonder?" Captain Sukin inquired. "Is it not your direct responsibility to care for order on the Dnieper Dam? Or do you want all American newspapers to trumpet about chaos on the Great Construction?"

Reluctantly, Katz put on his sheepskin jacket and followed the militia squad. That hated American ass, he was even glad his damn pants had been stolen, the pants he might have unbuttoned to sleep with his wife. He was not going to pass the complaint on to the militia despite the order to cater to all Mr. Winter's wishes. However, much in her style, Darya had the nerves to casually mention the matter to Sukin at the canteen, handing him the copy of Hugh Winter's letter. Whatever grudge she could bear against the gypsies, was beyond Haim's power of deduction.

The Superintendent climbed into the Ford AA beside Captain Sukin. The squad mounted into the trailer. They started for the Caucasus.

No need to observe political correctness, no obligation to sing propaganda songs. Whatever the ban, the Caucasus celebrates gypsy Christmas, and only January reigns under the blanket of minus 20 degrees Fahrenheit, disciplining the terrible Dnieper into a stock-still hulk of a mirror.

The Roma visit each other's tents, partake of the flour-and-fat soup, drink coffee made of dandelion roots. In the middle of the camp, a ruddy bonfire is a-rustle.

Romess Zareena caught a partridge, roasted it and stuffed a tin button into its belly, for lack of a traditional gold coin. Who will be lucky next year? A little boy squeals with joy, spitting out his tin fortune and brandishing it all over the camp. Other children chase him. Confidently, they cross the sandy beach patch and glide along the hard aspic of ice—it takes them seconds to reach the Glutton Rapid, jutting out like a harmless haystack. The children run on, up the ice-buried tide, past One too Much, its lupine teeth locked behind the deep-frozen gums of the river, past Schoolgirl Cliff, now no more deadly than a cottage stoop. The children chase the tin button winner on granite tops, adult swearing clad in their lucid, jingle-bell voices. The boy drops the tin button—the same color with ice and stone, and it is at once lost in the darkness.

Around the bonfire, the women shuffle a card pack, fan it out, peacock it up, garland it around the dishes. "What's on your heart, what is now, what was, what will be. New roads, new worlds… No!—please not nine of clubs, no, these are tainted cards, Zareena, your donkey must have pissed on them, bring me another deck."

Sergeant Sukin stops the Ford AA at the camp edge, a clothes line concealing him from sight. The gypsies hear the noise but don't let on it bother them on Christmas night.

"Shush-shush, militiamen, don't you see I'm listening to the horses?" says Rom Stepán, a bottle of moonshine in his hand. He is hiding behind a cart, so that a black stud and a bay mare can't see him. It is only at Christmas time you can hear horses gossip about their owner: whether they are satisfied with food and care, and the master's character, so that in the New Year a horse's life can be improved.

"Girl finds me fine, but Raven says he doesn't like the food," Stepán confides in the young militiaman. His face is in serious concern. "No wonder, you'd say the same if you'd been munching on rotten hay all year."

Rom Stepán steps out of the cart shadow. He is wearing the second pair of Winter's soiled-smoked jeans, a gift of respect to the future father-in-law from Rom Román. The old man takes two lumps of sugar out of his back pocket.

"Here, look at the Christmas treat for my sweethearts. What soft lips, what grateful eyes. Mind you, I won't even give this sugar to my own kids—it's only for my black gold, aye, and for my bay gold. Eat, eat, dearies, thank you for your truth."

Aza put Rom Román on her big dowry pillow, at a small fire by her tent. The girl sits sadly by his side, indifferent to camp's merrymaking. She watches her bridegroom toss, shudder, and twitch in fever. His fox-bitten wrist is swollen and red. It has been two weeks since he delivered the hides to the dam boss-woman. Two nights before, he took old Zareena's tent for Aza's and threw himself on the wrinkled body, waking up all the camp and setting it a-peal with laughter. Everybody took this for a bawdy joke. Yesterday, for no reason, Román swore at Aza terribly and hauled an anvil at his future father-in-law, whereas nobody had ever seen him even grumpy before. Now he is on the pillow, air around him falling apart in poisonous thorns, flogging his face. The songs he used to sing best in the camp now blow up his eardrums like hellhound barking. Aza brings a mug of water to his lips, but Román hits at it fiercely, his throat wrung by a spasm.

Illness is a given thing with the Roma, a doom not to be changed. It doesn't interrupt the camp's healthy dealings, even if the sick person is popular and loved. If it passes without a toll, thank God. If it takes a gypsy life, so be it.

Stepán turns to his eldest daughter, "Go have some fun, Aza. You can't help him anymore."

Aza stays rigidly seated, feeding the tent fire with more sticks.

The militiamen make their way to the shimmying epicenter of gypsy Christmas, the central bonfire wrapped in skirts, tip-tapped around by merry bare feet, bedanced and besung.

> *Birds of God know no labor,*
> *God's own Roma know no pain, All*
> *day long we dance and hover,*
> *Donkeys-horses neigh in hay.*

"Now, dirty parasites of the Soviet country, it's time to repent of your crimes," says Captain Sukin.

"What crimes, what crimes, militiamen?" chirp the women. "We live along, eat little, bother no one. Dance with us, militiamen, come taste our soup, drink our coffee."

"Have your fate foretold, young militiaman, such fierce eyes, such sure gait," says Zareena.

"Come here, Jewish man, drink moonshine with me," Rom Stepán beckons Katz, "Jews and gypsies are cousins in fate."

Haim feels eerie. He steps back towards the automobile, away from the warmth but less exposed to what he didn't want to be part of.

"Now you vermin of sabotage, who broke the rabbet fence, who stole American pants, who never stirred a hand to help build the dam? Take off at once what's not yours," ordered Sukin.

Rom Stepán takes off the jeans reluctantly, his gray oldmanhood peeping listlessly through the tatters of a shirt.

With clubs, the squad chases the camp of 200 gypsies in a bunch.

"And what the hell is this?" Captain Sukin points at Rom Román, who is deliriously beating about himself, cursing, half in Romani, half in Russian. "The fiend, too, has American pants on!"

"Leave him alone, militiaman, he's rabid, and his pants are rabid, too."

A gloved militiaman tries to catch Román by the pant cuffs but gets a punch in his face with the sick man's hard foot.

"Leave him alone, Ivan," says Captain Sukin, "or you'll catch the rabies, too."

The Captain straightens his shoulders. The squad lines up.

"Now you gypsies all hearken. For your black crimes,

for your incompatibility with the Soviet regime, you are banished from this land. Take your rags with you but leave the horses here. The rabid gypsy stays, he's no use. Cold will do it for us."

Like a flock of finches, with no resistance, the Roma surge off without touching the ground, still singing along. Stepán kisses the black stud and the bay mare goodbye and takes the dogged, sobbing Aza by her hand.

"We are the Roma folk," the old man coos in her ear, "we don't cling, we bear no grudge. God gave—God took—say thanks—forget, you will know many more men."

"Let him have my pillow at least," weeps the girl.

"It's your only dowry. You won't get another."

Flanked by the squad, the nomad crowd hovers along the bank, past the harmless rapids, past the digger camp and tilers' barracks, past Torgsin, skirting the great construction site. The militia men lead the black stud, the bay mare and three donkeys on harness. They will contribute to the reinforcement of the dam stables. At the end of the gypsy stream, Captain Sukin on Ford AA at the steering wheel, with Katz on the passenger seat.

"Ah, Superintendent, Superintendent, what a meek man, hid yourself in the bush as if they were none of your business," he chuckled, more chewing on his roll-up than smoking.

A girl rushes swiftly to the side and starts to run back. From the cargo load, a shot plummets, and the girl falls into the snow.

Katz winces, "Is it that necessary?"

Captain Sukin says nothing but gives Katz a strict, eloquent look.

At the railroad station, icy cargo boxcars take the whole gypsy camp in, tirelessly ai-ne-ne-ne-ing, Siberia—or heaven-bound. Small children cling to Rom Stepán, wiping their sobs on his gray chest and on the blanket covering his naked hips. Rom Stepán sheds his tears into their pates, "Our Aza is no more."

When Haim got back home in the small hours, Darya was absent, which frequent fact, for once in life, he registered indifferently, with an outskirt corner of his mind, its forefront all dappled and ragged with the night raid. Cousins in fate, he said to himself, putting his boots beside the primus stove to dry.

22.

The last turbine has been assembled. It is a shining behemoth snail, packed in scaffolds, swathed in algae of ropes. Workers as small as ants crawl all about it, sliding down, climbing up again. The industrial part of the great construction site is almost over, and Haim Katz envelops himself into the next demiurgic fervor—now health and beauty are duly in his paramount focus, which came in propitious for his mind to oust the insistent, irrevocable prospect of a bastard baby.

Thanks to the new Law of Five Ears of Wheat, there is enough money for health and beauty. The peasants are now allowed to possess no more than a handful of grain after harvesting—diligent militia and volunteer brigades take care of the law's enforcement. Should a hidden sack be unearthed in a barn, the brigades are authorized to shoot the culprits.

The Superintendent had a greenhouse and a garden built near the Machine Hall, "to meet the Great Helmsman in dignity." He phoned Massandra Botanical Garden and placed an order of a scope the garden had never had before and was never to receive afterwards. In two boxcars of a cargo train, magnolias, rhododendrons and orchids along with 500 young peaches and 700 mulberry trees traveled from the Crimea to Zap. His own palms rougher than tree bark, Haim moved from sapling to sapling to touch each fresh branch, each tender leaf, each blushing petal.

Apart from mere physical eye pleasure, beauty was to be raised to spiritual planes, the education and honing of which had actually been his wife's duty. They were not on speaking terms, not even on cursing terms. Haim thought that Darya's inglorious behavior forfeited her right to occupying her post. Anyway, in her eighth month of pregnancy, she was walking about bulged, soporific, and bleached, unable to attend to her job properly, and now, at the onset of the ninth month, she never leaves bed altogether, which is why Haim Katz overtook the responsibility for the Zap body and spirit.

For the well-being of the multi-thousand Dam and adjacent factories' staff, a new modern hospital appeared, albeit far away from the construction site but with an excellent obstetrics station for the new Soviet citizens: after Machine Hall, the second wonder of constructivist avant-garde. For spiritual development, two theaters were built, Marx Sound Movie and Gogol Drama. On the left bank of the Dnieper, unfolds a new Communard Settlement construction.

> To be eligible for residence in Communard Microdistrict, the dam personnel must prove to be willing to spend all their time in the commune and go home only for the night. For this, special sleeping cabins of five square feet with double beds are foreseen. Lavatories, showers, cloakrooms, laundries, kitchens—all the facilities—are exclusively communal.

—Haim Katz

The number of applications and supplications for residence at the Communard Microdistrict exceeds the number of available sleeping cabins by ten thousand.

"Another push, Comrade Katz, another push, I can see the head!" urges Dam Doctor Mandarinov.

"Don't breathe at me, Mandarinov, you're stealing my air!" yells Darya.

During her last contraction, she pulls at the doctor's left ear, nearly tearing it off. With a taut swish and a roily squirt, drenching the doctor's robe, Ex-Duchess shoots out a son.

Despite numerous invitations, Mandarinov refused to join the new hospital staff. In his facetious parlance, he explained that he would not like to lose touch with the heart of the dam whose beat he had been accompanying from the very start, but in truth, it was a much more material heart he wished to be close to, since the Waltz of Snowflakes, in unrequited affection.

Darya's labor began in a coup de force at summer solstice, at a temperature not much different from a furnace's, three weeks earlier than due. There was no way for her to benefit from the new excellent hospital. She had to be immediately brought to the Dam infirmary, her stomach an incongruous, bluish hump. Already dilated for the baby to pass, she was put on the same table where the Olivier salad stood six months ago, and where cookie Masha had a stillborn a week before.

The boy is red-haired and teal-eyed. He looks like Darya in miniature. It is not to decipher what other gene stuff the newborn is made of, and it would be beyond a noblewoman's dignity to wonder. The Head of Personnel gives her offspring a vacant look and closes her eyes.

Mandarinov sends the nurse away. His doctor's mask cast off, he washes the emptied body himself, a wet cloth dripping over her daisy freckles, over the subcutaneous blue streams.

"Register him Nathan," says Haim Katz, his lips pursed. "Thank God Mother Cypa didn't live to see this. Yes, I'm a weak man. I will give him my good last name although the chance he ever gets Jewish blood is through bedbugs." Haim must have forgotten about Aaron Garlic, but it is not Darya's intention to remind him.

"Since when has Katz been a good family name? Thank God Father Duke can't hear it," she says instead.

To no avail, Nathan is desperately trying to gain some milk from his mother. Little as Darya had generated, it all burned out in her breasts with a hiss. No wonder: it is no noblewoman's business to nurse. From cow's milk, Nathan turns ever redder with rash and anger.

Stock clerk and Dam painter Bogomole brings in some clean bedclothes.

The day before, Haim had the displeasure to sit for him full face in the conference hall, his eyes attempting to fix on some dust particles halfway between the painter and himself. Now Comrade Katz can easily avert his face and leave the room. Ex-Deacon still cannot understand why the powerful Superintendent would avoid meeting eyes with a petty employee.

"I could baptize the baby boy. He'll feel better after that," Bogomole whispers to Darya, pulling the pillowcase onto a hedgehog-prickly pillow.

"I was baptized by Patriarch Tikhon of Moscow himself, Deacon. What kind of shrill demotion you are offering me here! And you must be aware my husband is a Jew."

"Do you know how many Jews I baptized? And all of them were so happy after accepting Jesus—only once did I see a young chap with an indifferent face. The next day I found his cross in the ditch, but this Jew was an exception, and in very hot hell now, or will soon be."

"You'd better indulge in your smear-passion. It's my turn to sit for you today—there are square feet for you to cover!" Darya advises. "Tomorrow, it is Great Helmsman's turn, take his photo from The Pravda—and don't forget to depict all his pox furrows."

Vassili is ordered to augment the portraits to huge sizes for decorating the Alley of Enthusiasts, along which Comrade Stalin will be driven in his black shellproof Packard Twelve, in a cortège of shellproof Vauxhalls.

Armaïs Esaw-Yantz has brought Darya a stick of Hungarian salami and a head of Dutch cheese. As a store manager, he was not obliged to deliver the ration himself, but curiosity is tearing him apart.

"Is khe mine, is khe mine? Just tell me. Sons are an honor for an Armenian aristokrat, khoever they're by."

"Have you left your workplace to bellow around here?"

"If khe's mine, I promise to give khim my proud family

name, what did you kall this boy, Sathan?—Khe would be an Esaw-Yantz, and khow majestic it would sound!"

"Nathan Katz is majestic to tears all right," Darya replied, closing the door.

"Pardon me for a remark, but your ant's breasts, I didn't mind them in a straddle split but I don't really believe they kan produce milk," Armaïs shouts from the infirmary stoop. "I khave splendid Amerikan mock milk for infants in stock, khalf-price for you if khe's mine!"

Doctor Mandarinov ushers Cookie Masha in—to fetch her, he walked all the way to the digger camp, where the woman had to return. A thorough examination showed she was surprisingly STD-clean, and fusillading with unclaimed milk, so Darya Katz rewarded her once again, with a promotion to a wet nurse. The gain is mutual: Masha forever relieved of the cookie chore, and Darya of maternal role.

23.

"S-so, S-superintendent, I hear of grandiose success-ss. What a mighty achievement! All your own wit, grown on the yeas-s-t of your care, eh?"

Haim Katz is pale and at ho on the Headquarters phone.

"We are awaiting you, Iosif Viscerionovich, to look at it yourself!"

"Pity to s-say, s-so much to do, too much business-s, Haim. I don't like to break my promiss, I would love to come, but with all these enemies of the folk, I can't even breathe. But I'm s-sending an envoy to you, my right hand, Mikhail Ivanovich Kalinin. He will tell me everything. Are you all right with it?"

The kind tone of voice, this egalitarian apologizing question mark at the end, the high smile transmitted from the Kremlin, and Comrade Stalin's calling Katz by his first name—almost too much honor to bear.

Mikhail Kalinin's nickname is All-Soviet Alderman. His very low peasant descent and docile character guaranteed him safety under ubiquitous purges. He is a signing extension of Stalin's right hand for most of the documents—but in matters of high politics, he doesn't decide much, and nobody ever listens to him in the Politburo.

Mikhail Ivanovich Kalinin can't tell fouetté from pas-de-deux, but he loves ballerinas with all his elderly loins. When no ballerinas are available, milkmaids are almost as good as well as the concrete layeresses. The Great Helmsman affectionately calls him "All-Soviet Randy Goat."

Being Stalin's right hand is a strenuous task. It speeds up heartbeat and does telltale things to blood circulation. Wicked tongues say the All-Soviet Alderman tries to restore his potency by sitting down into a beehive. The bees bite his privates to make blood fill the cavernous cavity of the illustrious Politburo member.

The day before Kalinin's arrival, the Superintendent made sure the railway station Zaporozhye Main was cleaned from hundreds of peasants escaping from the Law of Five Ears of Wheat, bloated with starvation, faces greenish, many lying around like stacks of firewood, some still stirring, some fainted, some over the earthly fields.

The Alley of Enthusiasts is decorated with slogans and portraits the brush of Vassili Bogomole, on 400 thousand square feet, in a ton of gouache. Comrade Stalin's countenance is pink and smooth as a baby's. It measures 50 feet in height. Comrade Kalinin's head is 32 feet tall, Haim and Darya's twenty. Vassili spent a bucket of poison-green gouache to depict Darya's irises, and two men would have enough space to lie down on Haim's nose. In a more modest size of 20 feet, dozens of Dam Labor heroes are to behold, Nikolai and Petro heading the array.

A procession of black, shellproof Vauxhalls moves

slowly through the jubilant crowd. In the absence of Iosif Viscerionovich and his Packard Twelve, Kalinin's automobile comes first. The All-Union Alderman dons an astrakhan hat and a nimble goatee. He sits between Haim and Darya, who are given the honor of relating the high guest the story of epochal construction. The following vehicles contain Hugh Winter, Ukrainian Republic chieftains, renowned professors and journalists from all over the eager world. An obligatory member of NKVD occupies the front seat in each car.

"Here we pass our pride, the new Dam hospital with its excellent obstetrics station," Haim says with deliberate gusto. He doesn't fail to incinerate cyanine anger in Darya's glance at the memory of her own delivery, and she is already vexed enough. Her jacket is a plot of ever uglier ladies' fashion and blooper thumbs of the available seamstresses: the gray tweed cheap and coarse, the fronts of the double-breasted jacket askew, the lapels too low, flaps hanging like spaniel's ears.

The 40th anniversary came upon Darya in October, trampling her woman's confidence into the dust. Overnight, she watched her face turn sharp and sour. Crow's feet clawed the corners of her eyes and mouth. As a birthday present to herself, she uprooted the bathroom mirror and broke it against the stone floor.

She would have been glad to shine among all those newly arrived foreigners, some of them of considerable man-appeal. But Darya will shun contacts. To be just a quick-witted middle-aged interlocutor without making men realize they were being honored by the presence of a beauty would be too painful, too humiliating. However, the All-Union Alderman looks at her with caprine admiration: what a singular vixen, hair flaming red, and thin as a ballerina.

The escort stops at Zap Steel Plant. The high guests disembark and proceed inside, where they are shown the open hearth oven. The oven is fed with scrap metal. It is warmed by Dam power. Under the gazes of the high guests, a casting ladle approaches it. The hearth tips over, issuing the molten sunset of first steel.

The photographers hiss with their cameras non-stop. They find the striking difference of Winter and Katz much more interesting than the hearth: a hackneyed, nervous, fidgety Jew and the handsomely calm Viking, as broad as the Dnieper itself.

"What a pair, what a pair! A duet of great friends, fair and dun, the fathers of the Dam—Mr. Winter, Mr. Katz, give each other a hug!" the Times reporter shouts.

By now, the good-natured American has completely ousted his affair with Darya. He barely noticed she had had a baby, never assuming the possibility of his having anything to do with it. He readily reaches out to Katz, but the latter jumps away from Hugh like from a leper. Remembering his early love of cauldrons, he wishes to rather be in a stream of steel than in Winter's arms.

"Dramatic feud of two Dam fathers—Soviet Superintendent apparently reluctant to embrace the superiority of American professionalism," reported the Herald Tribune.

"A heart-rending rivalry over a woman, the beauteous propaganda dame of the dam. Her outfit is not exactly haute couture, but the invincible elegance shines through her every pore. It is said she belonged to higher aristocracy before the Revolution, and every pink-golden hair of hers betrays that," wrote the Sun.

The kitchen factory canteen is scrubbed with spirits. The tables are covered with white tablecloths. For months, the promoted Porko has been working away on Dam Triumph Menu, a happy marriage of simplicity and refinement that would at once bewitch the guests high and low. His key idea was to develop a proletarian answer to the Olivier Salad—genuinely Soviet, cheap and unprepossessing, but as impressive to a worker's palate as the original had been to noblemen's. He added and subtracted ingredients and counted the costs before the final recipe came to life.

Three hundred sacks of potatoes, four hundred bunches of carrots, five hundred eggs, the beef of ten cows; ten pounds of onions, a keg of pickles: blend with a hundred cans of green peas and lubricate all this by "Drowned Glutton" mayonnaise.

Not only will the recipe outlive Cook Porko without so much as an honorable mention, it will outlive the Soviet Union itself, pillaged from Dam Celebration in all map directions, retaining the old Olivier name it defiled (the seminal French chef is tired of turning in his grave, for there is no sign of people's ever leaving the fake recipe alone). They cut the cubes and will cut the cubes for every festivity, from Moscow to the smallest pimple of a village, decades and decades hence.

The doors of the canteen swing open. The NKVD men assign the rest to their places. Once Kalinin gives a sign, everybody attacks food and drink, of which there is abundance: good vodka and whisky and decent table wine.

Professors, renowned journalists, and high Communist Party figures toast simple workers in democratic endearment. High officials talk and joke with concrete layer heroines and brigade she-cookies. Everything teems and mingles.

Nikolai and Petro push their way to Mikhail Kalinin.

"Heloes of the Dam are always welcome!" Kalinin winks at the pair, noticing Medals of Soviet Labor on their lapels. "I hope you also had some fun. They say dam women are as good in bed as on the constluction site?"

"We don't complain, Comrade Kalinin, but socialist industry is more on our minds than love—first diggin', then friggin'," replies Nikolai.

"And dances? Do you have dance evenings in the wolkers club?"

"Ah what dances, Comrade Kalinin, we were so tired all the time that we didn't even have pep to lay our Masha's pipe at night, but now she's been taken away from us to nurse the head of Propaganda's baby—lucky little bastard, he gets all of her tits now."

Nikolai elbows Petro in the rib.

"Ah, we are simple people, Comrade Kalinin," he says, "but our bosses, they have more time for fun."

Nikolai and Petro interrupt each other, take turns parodying waltzes and quadrilles. Nikolai depicts a female shape and spins with his fingers in the air to depict embroidery and lace. Kalinin's goatee jumps excitedly. He pats both dam heroes on their shoulders and returns to the Headquarters table, giving credit to some notable female rears on the way. He sits down next to Darya.

"Comlade Katz, you look like a ballelina, and they say you dance almost as well! Can you show me a fouetté, or shall we do a pas-de-deux on this table? You can put on that gown the whole dam is talking about, and then take it off! Dance for me and you will be safe flom plison—folever."

"Comrade Kalinin, I am very sorry, but I am not prepared for this honor. I would take you to the greenhouse and pay you my reverence amongst the orchids, but my husband has not ordered any beehive. There's not a single beehive on the Dam," Darya replies.

Kalinin's goatee sharpens. He flushes and retreats several tables back into the depth of the canteen. In a second, he is immersed into a very tactile conversation with the ex-she-cookie Masha, to whose left breast little Nathan is absorbedly helping himself.

"Let's see if Comlade Supelintendent can olganize a plivate boat fol us, only you, me and my loyal bodyguald Fedka. Fedka will hold the baby, too."

Darya leaves the party much earlier than the protocol prescribes. In the window, she sees Haim's agitated profile. He is having a time of his life, proud and obviously glad she is gone. Hugh is posing against the fireworks, letting himself be hugged by sundry workers. At home his she-beetle awaits him patiently, too timid to even mingle with the crowd.

Dam Triumph night boat tour has started, with sparklers in each boat. Darya marches away from the Dnieper. She does not see herself in the picture she helped create, to which she had even given a name.

From her Father's villa, 18 and in a dizzily daring bathing suit, she runs to the beach, her hair the color of the new-born sun. On the shore, an angular, ugly young Jew is devouring cherry jam with a big spoon right out of the jar. He is a lodger in someone's dacha attic and they say in Massandra he is a poet, Osip Mandelshtam. The spoon poises in the air, of course, when he sees Darya, and his uncouth features light up. ("No, I'd better sleep with a goat," she says proudly to herself and then to all her Massandra friends.)

The poem Darya caught in Mandelshtam's eyes materialized in the Northern Lily magazine, in the same issue Darya had hers published.

Behind the cowl of the palace,
Under the foam of blooming gardens,
There is a land inside my eyelids,
In this land you will be my spouse.

The date and place left no doubt about the addressee. This did not make her desire the ugly poet any more, but before she could realize it, she kissed his name on the gray page.

24.

The tuff wall of the magnificent Machine Hall at 8:00 AM, the pink trinity of stone, hair, and dawn. "This picture deserves the brush of a painter," or in words simpler put, Captain Sukin's mind formed an impression of his own installation, the piled models in artistic disarray. He had no idea of Klimt, or of Schiele, who had already painted such pictures, much in the same sunrise palette.

Sukin even felt somewhat honored to deal with the Head of Propaganda for the fantastic impudence of the woman, whose scale of transgression he admired. She was really royally guilty, unlike her peevish husband. The high order was to conduct the procedure swiftly, top secret, without informing the Superintendent, so as not to disquieten him without need.

There had been no trace of fear, not even a sign of reluctance on her face, teal eyes cold and indifferent. The Captain single-handedly dealt with this big dam she-bird, while his subordinates took care of the rest: six items of men-vermin, of different calibers and sizes. They were a pitiful sight: the drink-desiccated, sobbing welder, the doctor who tried to hold hands with the woman, embarrassing the executive squad, so they had to deal with him quick to stop the disgrace; the swearing plumber; the crest-fallen cook; the squat man, cackling deliriously in Armenian. Only the clumsy painter-carpenter, the former priest, had more of a human face on. He prayed and sang in a handsome bass, so that the squad even lingered a bit.

Against the common, unfair opinion, Sukin didn't find his work pleasurable at all, and he never let his squad slide into the macabre, as some execution captains he had heard of. He strictly forbade anything more than the practical, necessary confiscation of sturdy footwear or clothing items for militia stocks. Sukin wouldn't let the militia broads take hold of Darya Katz's confiscated ball dress. He followed it through to the new Gogol Theatre, where it would make a jewel of the wardrobe, the only problem being is its bird size—but then the canny proletarian actresses can drape the open corset clasps with knit shawls. As for the black, very fashionable shoes, well, their size was exactly his wife's.

The Captain filled out the protocol of execution, in alphabetical order, which he prided himself in arranging at a lightning speed.

October 12th, 1932

V. Bogomole, G. Eelovy, A. Esaw-Yantz, D. Katz,

B. Mandarinov, M. Porko, S. Ticklick

Executed by firing squad under the guidance of Captain Ivan Sukin

Sentence carried out at 7 AM

Corpses passed on to the digger brigade for burial

The sentence of Esaw-Yantz was different form the rest of his co-murderees. The militia hadn't even suspected any connection, for Armaïs had successfully destroyed all traces of ball-related dealings. Instead, he was accused of espionage and commissioned mass murder on behalf of American imperialism, having been caught hot-handed for preparations to poison Soviet dam babies, with an irrefutable proof of 200 identical acid-green foreign-manufactured cans in the warehouse of Torgsin, with a baby face on them, the poison name Similac. All the cans contained cruelly sweet white powder. Good the Armenian fiend hadn't managed to put his horrible plot into practice.

In his bunkhouse, the militia found no further evidence of criminal activity or foreign currency. The Esaw-Yantz nesting-doll of a wife had hidden a pickle can inside her spacious canal of life. Inside the pickle can, there was a fat roll of American dollar banknotes, 1,500 to be exact: providently, for the future education of the Armenian Lautrec and the future best doctor of female laps.

Pink sun is rising in the October sky, promising a windy day. The digger brigade's last assignment is burying the executed gang.

"The ground is so hard, so difficult to dig!"

"Load'em on a cart, cover with burlap, push along," Nikolai commands.

"They are building a new block for married dam workers, and we will live in a separate room, five square feet, all for Masha and me!" says Petro, "I asked her to marry me, and she accepted."

"You unscrupulous beast! If I had proposed to Masha, she would have fainted with joy, only I can't marry a fuck latrine, which not even Comrade Kalinin's milt can redeem, and because of my high principles I will have to go on living in the bunkhouse."

"But I do like Masha well enough, I make her feel good,

and you have always liked Comrade Katz, but now she is here in the cart, red-dead as a doornail because of you."

"Easy on, Prince Myshkin, remember you helped me along."

They pull the cart all along the digger camp, the builder camp, the welder camp, towards the construction site of the New Communard Microdistict. After the dam was finished, the Superintendent lowered his demands, released his relentless control grip, so the builders would not start work before ten in the morning.

"Is this where your block of flats will stand?" asks Nikolai. "Now let's fertilize your future house a bit, so you thrive and multiply."

Nikolai wheels the cart towards the foundation and lets its contents fall. Then he tilts the cistern full of fresh concrete into the cavity, "Wouldn't you like, lazy bone, to kill two birds with one stone? No digging and better than buried: entombed."

25.

"What a meek man you are, Comrade Katz," said Captain Sukin the next day, throwing a pile of protocols onto the desk before Haim's eyes. "Harbored a snake on your chest and never noticed? What speedy case processing, directly from Moscow. What signatures under the sentence! Shame-disgrace, Comrade Katz."

Sukin put a file on the table and opened it with a flourish. He read, savoring every word:

Darya Katz, née Duchess Voronchina. Prepared and carried out an anti-communist plot. Ignoring the state ban on religion, indulged in the degenerate ritual of the so-called Christmas. Let out the ailing heroes of the dam from the infirmary, depriving them of the right to medical care. Held a ferocious sex orgy, copulating perversely in standing, in chronological order: with cook Porko, Feldsher Mandarinov, welder Gleb Eelovy, carpenter Bogomole, plumber Ticklick. Expressed contempt to the Soviet Army by abusing its sacred power represented by the tin effigy of its soldier. Accused of High Treason. The said politically unstable accomplices accused of Insidious Lechery and Sabotage. All six sentenced to capital punishment.

Haim lowered his head, clutching the leather of his boot.

"And here is what I have for you," Sukin went on. "Negligent malpractice, criminal connivance, aiding and abetting an anti-Soviet plot, espionage for Zionist Palestine." If you were a simple worker, I could guarantee your life—maybe ten to 20 years of GULAG, but you were on such a high post. Comrade Stalin and Comrade Kalinin are very disappointed you let them down. I advise you to sign now—you will sign anyway, but after much muscle kerfuffle you certainly don't want."

"Comrade Sukin," Katz reached his sandpaper-rough palms towards Captain in dismay, "These hands have touched every single pebble, every single nail on this dam—look around—I made it all, I did!"

"You might have used your hands well, but your eyes—you kept them closed all the way."

"Where is my wife?" Katz asked in a low voice.

"Ah, what's the difference—say good-bye and good riddance."

Sukin gave Haim's high boots an appraising, conspiratorial wink—his shoe size seemed the same as the Superintendent's—and handed Haim a pen. The first order had been to transport Superintendent Katz to Moscow for a proper trial, but transporting Katz to the capital city would have been a logistic nightmare. In a week, the order was replaced by a more reasonable version to be carried out locally.

In the Ford AA, they made a lap of honor around the majesty of the finished Dnieper Dam and drove farther in the direction of the gypsy-free Caucasus patch. The car stopped under an oak-tree facing the ex-Glutton Rapid, now a mere harmless mound in the middle of the river. The Superintendent's privilege was to be treated separately and discreetly.

"Leave your boots in the automobile, Comrade Katz," ordered Sukin. "You won't need them anymore."

Two militia women, Sergeant and Private, came to the Headquarters barrack to pick up the children. Nathan was quiet and easy to handle, but Mania fought fiercely. Clutching her rag doll (half of its eyelashes fallen out, one shoe), she bit the Private woman's finger. The Sergeant woman tried to take the unhygienic rag away, but Mania bit again, her teeth perforating the uniform coat, tearing out a piece of Sergeant's forearm flesh. Groaning with pain, the women threw off their coats and surrounded Mania. They managed to wrap her in, muffling her together with the rag doll, forever in her iron grit. In short order, the children were safely dispatched to Dam Juvenile Detention Cell, and both militiawomen rushed to the infirmary to get immunization against rabies. The infirmary appeared empty of personnel, for no replacement had yet been found for the freshly executed Doctor Mandarinov, which was not a big issue: the Soviet militiamen and militiawomen would not be deterred from giving themselves a syringe shot. However, all the medicine bottles were labeled in Latin, and none of them had Russian words "against rabies" on it, so the women took out their nickel-barreled revolvers and discharged their displeasure on the inscrutable medicine cabinet. The Sergeant mounted a black gypsy stud and the Private got on a bay gypsy mare. They left for the faraway new modern hospital, an anxious hour's ride.

26.

"If it is a boy, let him be Solomon, if a girl, let her be Winona," Rosa muses. She hopes the baby will be blond with blue eyes. She covers the furniture with blankets. The bedroom is full of expensive leather suitcases.

"Good-bye, skinny bourgeois, hello fat bourgeois," she murmurs, replacing the used-up Nennen shaving cream with the new tube for the last time.

"Good-bye, kosher butcher, she says," wiping the Gillette razor. Then she dares her last luxury, knowing that Hugh would not mind even if he noticed: into a tiny empty bottle that once contained iodine, she pours out some 4711 from the golden-friezed, dark turquoise flask—to store the adored perfume, to keep her lover a little longer beside her when he is gone, to last her the months before she got a little living copy of him to raise.

High rise the chimneys, black billows the smoke. The wild blue hair of the river has been groomed by a huge dam comb, 200 feet high and 3,000 feet wide. The rapids were irrevocably flooded, and the river put on weight. It bulged, slow-cow, bulky, swallowing the adjacent villages, and its stone teats disappeared entirely under the blue meat. Energy-giving saliva froths between the white teeth of the piers. With a capacity of 1,500 megawatts, it easily feeds the Steel-Aluminum Plant and Coke-Abrasive Factories as well as the Motor Works.

The Communard Microdistrict proved too cutting edge for dam minds. The residents liked to spend time together, playing cards, drinking and fighting, but nobody felt responsible for cleaning the communal lavatories, bathrooms, and kitchens, which reached the state of miasmatic, roach-teeming insanitation in no time. However, people's atavistic pining to possess their progeny proved obnoxiously incorrigible. They dodged giving the children away to the institutions, concealing their existence since birth, hiding them in the sleeping cabins, growth-stunted like tundra birches. No punishments helped. Tacitly, the project was closed, and the failed Communards were allowed to live as they pleased.

Instead of the sleeping cabins, stout tiled houses with high ceilings and spacious rooms came into vogue. The city was booming. Film companies came to shoot movies about the water wonder of technology, with a healthy infusion of love tales against the background of toiling heroism: between a notable welder and a cheerful concrete layeress, or between an honest carpenter and a devoted milkmaid. One such movie even displayed no less than a lip kissing scene.

The whole country took to shortening the name of Zaporozhye to the succinct, dynamic Zap.

On a business trip in Moscow, a Dam factory employee would be asked, "Where do you come from?" "From Zap," would be the reply, casual but full of pride.

"Who doesn't know Zap?" a Muscovite would smile respectfully, without a trace of condescension to provincials. "Stronghold of the country, on the verve of new times!"

Rosa had her baby in the full-fledged Dam hospital equipped to the latest world standards, the obstetrics department a miracle of medical state-of-the-art. Hugh had left for America a week before her delivery. His mission was over, the Zap chapter closed. Unexpectedly though, he had kindly acquiesced to Rosa's registering his biological offspring to come, whether Solomon or Winona, under his cold last name. He thought better of importing anything foreign to America. Ideal as a mistress, who knows what pranks this woman would develop as a wife. Meanwhile, Hoover Dam was awaiting his expertise in the Black Canyon of the Colorado River, and a much mightier dam than the Dnieper's it was going to be.

Journalists report that nowhere in the world have they seen orphans happier than at the Jewish orphanage in Odessa. Mania and little Nathan like their new home. They wear feeble but neat clothes. Almost always, they have enough food, which they grow in the garden themselves: potatoes, carrots, cabbages, onions. There is also an apple tree, a cherry tree, and a bed of white roses. In winter the children paint, craft, and sing every day. On cold evenings, they are read Adventures of Menahem-Mendl.

At 14, no trace is left of the bestial urchin Mania. The girl enjoys the benign adult attention of which she was so long deprived. She has learned some non-dam, literary Russian and read all Leo Tolstoy's stories for children. She is very musical, too, and a pedagogical talent is definitely unfurling in her dealings with younger fosterlings, so at least a piano teacher's career is being promised to her.

Unfortunately, against the principles of communist sharing, Mania doesn't let other girls play with her rag doll: cleaned, patched and mended, it rests in her bedside table, "for my future daughter." Fortunately, tutor Zelda

Zinovievna knows better than to combat this only residual character flaw.

By and by, the orphans discover the joys of cursive writing. Zelda Zinovievna likes to give the pupils short, funny dictations:

> A little Jewish kitten Basya is very playful. She awaits her Jewish masters from work impatiently because they always bring her some wonderful blood sausage from the butcher's—the sausage they love to eat themselves. On Saturday, Basya's masters go to work happily, and when they come home, they roast tasty pork.

The teal-eyed, red-haired Nathan is quiet, serious, solemn, a perfectionist. It is joked he will grow up to become Director of Blacking Factory in Moscow.

The Katzes children have friends in the asylum, siblings Dod and Sheila, whose parents died of typhus. Dod boasts that their father was the best tailor in the world and now he sews suits for Comrade God.

"But Zelda Zinovievna says there is no Comrade God whatsoever," argues little Nathan.

"Ah, your Zelda Zinovievna, she doesn't know a thing."

ABOUT THE AUTHOR

Svetlana Lavochkina is a Ukrainian-born novelist, poet and poetry translator, now residing in Germany. In 2013, *Dam Duchess* was chosen runner-up in the Paris Literary Prize, sponsored by Shakespeare and Company and the De Groot Foundation. Her debut novel, *Zap* (Whiskey Tit, 2017),was shortlisted for Tibor & Jones Pageturner Prize 2015. Svetlana's work has been widely published in the US and Europe. Her work has appeared in *AGNI, New Humanist, POEM, Witness, Straylight, Circumference, Superstition Review, Sixfold, Drunken Boat* and elsewhere.

ABOUT THE PUBLISHER

Whisk(e)y Tit is committed to restoring degradation and degeneracy to the literary arts. We work with authors who are unwilling to sacrifice intellectual rigor, unrelenting playfulness, and visual beauty in our literary pursuits, often leading to texts that would otherwise be abandoned in today's largely homogenized literary landscape. In a world governed by idiocy, our commitment to these principles is an act of civil service and civil disobedience alike.